PERLE
OF
LOVE

PERLE
OF
LOVE

A Once Upon Academy Story
Book 2

Perle & Zeke

MARIE LONG

Perle of Love
(Once Upon Academy: Perle & Zeke, Book 2)

Published by Chikara Press

Cover design by Claire Holt (Luminescence Covers)
www.luminescencecovers.com

Printed in the United States of America

10 9 8 7 6 5 4 3 2 1

ISBN: 978-1-7364913-9-3 (paperback)
ISBN: 978-1-960253-00-2 (eBook)

PERLE

OF

LOVE

CHAPTER 1

ZEKE WOLFSON GAZED UP AT the massive Tudor-style architecture of Once Upon Academy's main building. The muffled sounds of excited voices warned him that classes were between sessions. Clenching his jaw, he strode along the cobblestone walkway and up the shallow steps leading into the building. He had been hoping today would be an easy day.

Stately gargoyle sentinels perched on tall pillars watched from above as Zeke entered the academy's grand entrance. A mob of students bustling to and from their classes parted like a wave around him. A few students converged in small groups, muttering. Zeke's keen wolf hearing picked up his name in their hushed gossip about the Headmistress's 'favorite enforcer' getting called into her office. He wasn't surprised. Zeke was one of the academy's Resident Assistants, and he was often the subject of his peers' conversations after an incident occurred. His past heroics for OUA didn't seem to better his reputation. Zeke's frown warned the annoying gossipers not to try his patience.

He had hoped to spend the day wandering the academy's campus, breaking up petty arguments, giving prospective students the grand tour of all his favorite hangout spots, or guiding bewildered visitors around the campus—but a half-hour ago, he had received a summons.

Instead of enjoying the day, he was now on the top floor of the main building, standing before the closed double doors of the Headmistress's office. The noise of the students from the main floor was a dull buzz, and through the door he heard the Headmistress giving a stern lecture to whoever the miscreant was this time. Just last week, Zeke had delivered to the Headmistress a couple of knuckleheads who were spell-dueling outside of the school's designated area. An 'easy day' was wishful thinking, he realized, especially as the end of the school year neared. Zeke knocked on the ornate wooden doors in a special sequence that he and the Headmistress shared, and then quietly let himself in.

He closed the door behind him, leaned against the frame, and looked ahead. Standing before the Headmistress was a sophomore trickster named Margaret Feathersby. It appeared the young illusionist's latest infraction was deciding to turn the sconces in one of the lecture halls into giant cockroaches. Ms. Darling's Literature class had been sent into chaos.

Crossing his arms, Zeke's focus drifted past Margaret to the Headmistress's massive mahogany desk. It was covered with thick magical tomes, stacks of papers, and odd trinkets. Amid the items, placed at the corner of the desk, was the Headmistress's most prized possession: a smooth, perfectly shaped, bright-red apple. Zeke looked away.

Margaret was keeping her head lowered, strands of curly brown hair concealing parts of her soft face. She nervously twirled a loose black thread of her pleated skirt with her slender fingers.

Zeke wrinkled his nose. The fear the young illusionist radiated was an overpowering scent to his wolf senses. It reminded him of his own experience when he'd first arrived at Once Upon Academy. He had been angry at the world and angry at himself. But more than anything, he had been terrified, afraid of the unknown. All because of what he was—*who* he was: a son of the Big Bad Wolf. Feared by his peers, he was an outcast and destined to be alone.

The Headmistress's almond-colored eyes cast a fierce gaze upon Margaret. Her rose-red lips formed a thin line as she placed a silver ring on the desk and slid it forward.

Margaret's gaze locked on the ring, and her eyes widened. "No..." she muttered. The smell of her fear flooded Zeke's senses.

"You give me no choice but to enact the Ring of Nullification," the Headmistress declared. "You will wear it for three days. Additionally, you will be assigned cleaning duties at the horse stables and the first floors of the dormitories."

Zeke grimaced. A student caught wearing the Ring of Nullification would be subject to ridicule, embarrassment, and gossip amongst their peers. It was considered the ultimate insult to a magical being, as the ring prevented its bearer from using their powers.

Even worse than the shame, however, was the misery of wearing the thing. His heart pounded at the mere thought of experiencing the ring's qualities. For his entire tenure at the school, Zeke had only worn the ring once, and that was more than enough. The feeling of being unable to use his powers had frightened him. While he wore that ring, he was vulnerable, submissive, and helpless—the very things his family had told him he was and the very things he'd sworn he'd never become. He'd earned the punishment when he got into a physical fight with a senior student and used his shifter powers. The Evocation student had needed two days in the infirmary to heal.

For that incident, he was nearly expelled from Once Upon Academy. Thankfully, the Headmistress, in all of her wisdom and patience, was generous and forgiving. She believed in second chances, even for someone like him. It was a lesson learned, and one he would never forget.

Margaret looked at the ring, then chewed her bottom lip. "Oh, please, Headmistress. I'm sorry, I won't do it again, I promise!" she whimpered, folding her hands pleadingly. "Please, not the Ring, *please*! I beg you!"

The Headmistress stood from her high-backed chair and straightened, folding her hands at her waist. She looked down on Margaret, pinning her with a piercing, icy-cold and declared, "We have rules in place for a reason. The safety of this school and its students are my highest priorities. This is the third time in a month we are having this conversation. I hoped that by now you would have enough discipline to utilize your abilities in your studies, rather than using them to disrupt your peers. This matter is settled. Put on the ring."

Margaret hesitated, then slowly picked up the ring. Frowning, she examined it. Zeke remembered every aspect of that dreaded ring—its smooth silvery surface, the etched runes, its metallic smell. For a moment, he saw himself struggling to make himself put it on, the same way Margaret was stalling.

Margaret exhaled a deep breath, her shoulders slumping with acceptance. She slowly slipped the ring onto her right finger. A faint, purple glow emanated from the runes, and then disappeared.

"Three days, Ms. Feathersby," the Headmistress reminded. "If there is another offense, the days will be extended. Now, then," she pointed to the door, "you're dismissed. Mr. Wolfson will escort you to the stables."

At the sound of his formal name, Zeke perked up. He pushed off the doorframe and strode over to Margaret, who remained standing with a defeated expression on her pale face. He grunted and beckoned her with a firm head gesture. Margaret turned to him, her bottom lip quivering.

He chanced one glance at her right hand, and then turned away, heading for the exit. He was about to pull open the double doors when he heard the sound of wood scraping against stone behind him, and the sound of hurried footsteps approaching.

Zeke looked over his shoulder. A middle-aged female attendant dressed in purple robes, branded with OUA's crest on the front, rushed out from a side entrance that led from a descending stairwell. Her two long golden braids wildly swung behind her as she ran to the Headmistress's side.

"Headmistress!"

The Headmistress raised a thin, dark eyebrow.

"You're needed... in the summoning chambers... at once!" the woman said between her panting.

Concern flashed across the Headmistress's face before quickly returning to her icy demeanor. She strode to the doorway, stopped, and looked over her shoulder at Zeke. "Mr. Wolfson," she instructed, "please return as soon as you have taken care of Ms. Feathersby. I have another job for you." With that, she turned and disappeared down the stairwell with her assistant.

Zeke clenched his jaw as the door silently slid shut behind the departing women. He wondered what sort of new job she had in store for him this time, or if it had anything to do with her sudden departure. Working for the Headmistress had its ups and downs, but he did enjoy staying busy. OUA was his home, and the Headmistress was one of the few friends he had. She made him feel needed, wanted, and secure. Under her tutelage, he was learning to control his temper.

He and Margaret exited the office, Margaret trailing a few paces behind him. He didn't need to see her to know she was there. His sharp senses picked up the trickster's soft, gliding steps and the scent of her fear.

They left the main building through a side door and traveled a short distance through a patch of enchanted woods. When they emerged in a clearing, they saw the campus barn and stables. Horses of all shapes, sizes, and colors were kept here—mostly for the Riding and Equestrian classes. Zeke felt himself tense as they neared the main stable. He met the gaze of a white mare.

She snorted and whinnied, moving around in her stall with a nervous shuffle. Zeke sighed and looked away, wishing that he didn't always inspire fear in prey animals.

Margaret took one look at the horses and then grimaced. "Zeke… C-Can't you talk to the Headmistress and see about lessening my punishment?"

"You know I can't do that," he replied bluntly.

"But I was only playing around. I would never hurt anyone. You of all people would understand, right?" She regarded him with hopeful eyes.

"You can't expect to play these tricks and not get caught. Anyway, you're lucky it's just for three days."

Margaret released a drawn-out groan. "Ugh! One day is awful enough, much less three! What a nightmare…"

He snorted. "I had to wear that thing for a *week*, so don't whine to me about a nightmare." He gave her a stern look that told her the conversation was over.

Cringing, Margaret fell silent and trudged toward the stable. One of the keepers, a husky older gentleman, was hard at work cleaning out the stalls. Crossing his arms, Zeke watched and waited. He would ensure that his task was completed before he left. Margaret joined the keeper and chatted with him a few moments. Then, she gingerly picked up a shovel and glanced over her shoulder, casting Zeke a sour look. He fought down an amused smile as she entered one of the empty stalls and began mucking it out.

Satisfied that Margaret was taken care of, Zeke returned to the main building. Anxiety rose in his chest as he thought about the Headmistress's mysterious next task. She saw something special in him that he didn't see in himself. She'd shown him as much earlier in the year when she supported him in his quest to defeat an evil sorceress. Attempting to resist the sorceress's powers, her magical beasts, and using his shifter powers to protect his new friends had nearly cost him his life. He was hailed a hero of the school, and even now, he still didn't feel comfortable with that—seemingly, neither did his peers.

He knocked on the Headmistress's office door and let himself in. He noticed the room was still empty, and frowned. It appeared the Headmistress still hadn't returned from her impromptu meeting. Looking toward the Headmistress's desk, Zeke considered coming back later, instead of waiting here alone. But the last thing he needed was to invoke her wrath for not heeding her summons. After several moments, Zeke finally conceded and approached the desk.

What sort of urgent matter could have made her run off like that? he wondered as he took a seat in one of the high-backed chairs in front of her desk.

He scanned the room. His gaze locked on a side door that was open a crack. It was the same one that descended into the dark, narrow staircase the attendant had appeared from earlier. Curious, he rubbed his chin. He'd noticed the door to that hidden room many times, but never had he'd seen it opened. *What's down there, anyway?* His heart pounded. He was venturing into an area of the Headmistress's office he had never been.

He approached the door, slid it all the way open, and stared into the pitch-blackness to allow his wolf sight time to adjust. Once he could see the steps clearly, he noticed they spiraled down past his line of sight. He took a deep breath, filling his lungs with the cold, humid air wrought with the mixed scents of mildew and old stone. His ears perked at the echo of several mixed voices talking and chanting below him. He puffed out his chest, allowing his wolf's courage to calm his mind, and then began his descent.

Zeke ran his hand along the rough stone walls as he travelled deeper into the unknown depths. A shimmer of light danced across the walls. His steps turned cautious. The darkness of the stairwell eventually opened up into a blue-lighted chamber.

He pressed his back against the wall and peered around the edge. A large room, three times the size of the Headmistress's office, opened in front of him. A group of purple-robed men and women stood around a large table, staring at a thick, closed tome set in the middle. The Headmistress stood at the head of the table, looking intently toward the book. Zeke focused on the book—his eyes widened as he recognized the rose image on the book's front cover.

His breath hitched, and a shiver ran through his body when he realized it was the enchanted tome of runes—the cause of all the trouble that happened around the school several months ago. His friend and fellow student, Perle Durand, had inadvertently obtained it from an evil sorceress. With Zeke's help, however, they were able to contain the dark magic.

The assistants, in ritualistic sequence, cast a variety of spells on the book. The prismatic array of colors and visual effects from the attendants' spells were strange and unfamiliar to him. He was a shifter, and therefore didn't follow the traditional path of magic comprised of incantations and enchantments. Frozen, he remained at the base of the stairs, watching with interest, thankful that no one seemed to be aware of his presence.

The Headmistress uttered phrases in a language that sounded like gibberish to his ears. He had a hard time understanding the nature of his own shifter powers, much less other forms of magic.

The Headmistress extended her hand toward the book, and it slid across the table toward her as if her hand were a magnet. The book stopped in front of her. A wave of gasps and murmurs swept through the chamber from the wary assistants.

"At last," the Headmistress said in a relieved voice. "I think we may have finally unlocked her secret..." She slowly placed her hand on the book.

Reflexively, as if reacting to her touch, a bright, orange-yellow glow emanated from the book. Suddenly, beams of golden light shot in all directions from the book. Everyone ducked and scrambled away from the table. The book rose on its own accord, hovering in mid-air, the beams of light continuing to shoot everywhere about the room.

"Look out!" a male assistant shouted as he dashed under the table.

The Headmistress rushed behind a narrow support column as a beam of light caught the hem of her dress, searing a small hole in the purple fabric.

Zeke stiffened. *She's in trouble!* His wolf instinctively wanted to protect the Headmistress, but he was also aware of the unknown danger of the hovering book.

He crouched low and concentrated, allowing his body to expand as he shifted into his wolf form. His transformation complete, he focused on the chaos once more with his newfound senses. He tried to analyze the light beams carefully in case they moved in a specific pattern, but they were as erratic as his own nerves. With a grunt, he bolted into the room, using the incredible speed and agility his wolf form provided to dodge and duck around the incoming beams as he made his way to the column where the Headmistress was hiding.

The Headmistress widened her eyes. "Zeke! What are you doing? Get out of here now!"

The pang of alarm in the Headmistress's voice gave him pause as he panted behind the column next to her. Part of him felt obliged to obey, but his wolf empowered him to remain. He shook his head slowly.

Protect the Headmistress at all costs.

"I said go! That is an order!" she barked.

His heart pounded faster. The urgency and forcefulness in her voice was enough to sway his wolf. *She is the Alpha.*

He launched himself away from the column toward the stairs, almost falling as his thick paws slipped on the polished stone floor. Scrambling to keep his balance, he raced back the way he came. He was almost to the staircase when a terrible shock suddenly struck him on his tail. A flash of pain seared through him hotter than fire, cutting sharper than any knife.

He let out a painful howl and felt his legs give way. He slid across the floor and hit the bottom step with a resounding thud. He tried to stand, but his body refused to obey his commands.

I... I can't move! Why can't I move?

His eyelids drooped as he fought to stay conscious. The screams and shouts of the attendants, the crumbling sounds of the stone walls, and the thundering of panicked footsteps echoed in his frazzled mind until he succumbed to the numbness sweeping over his senses. The world around him went black and deathly silent.

CHAPTER 2

PERLE DURAND ASSESSED THE wooden dummy, focusing on the tiny white target on its forehead. This was it. Her final exam. Her one and only attempt to flawlessly cast all seven of the Evocation spells that she had learned in her first year.

The incident several months ago with Tilda, the dark illusionist who had endangered the school with her evil magical beings, had tested the limits of Perle's magical abilities. After Tilda's defeat, Perle and her friends were revered amongst their peers. Some students looked to her for tutoring and advice. The added pressure made Perle strive for perfection in her own spellcasting. Too many people were counting on her now. She couldn't fail them, just as she couldn't fail her test.

Perle felt the eyes of her peers bearing down on her as she steadied her gaze on the wooden dummy. The spell had to be executed flawlessly. Her anxiety felt like a giant boulder resting on her chest.

She took several deep breaths. She desperately wished her cat—her familiar—Nuit was at her side, sending his calming, empathic vibes to her mind. But he was confined in her dorm until Familiars class later that day. Evocation was a class focused solely on one's singular magical ability, without the use of familiars or other outside forces.

"Ms. Durand," Mistress Fitcher, the Evocation professor's voice tore through the intense silence that filled the medium-sized, two-tiered seating classroom. "Remember, I am looking for accuracy and precision. Do not hesitate."

Perle nodded and inhaled deeply through her nose. The scent of aged mahogany that made up the classroom's interior eased her nervousness. Her gaze drew away from the white target and locked on the center of the dummy's chest.

Small target. Center. You see everything, she mentally chanted from her previous lectures.

This test had a few tricks of its own. The white target was a distraction, as Perle had seen from the other students' less-than-accurate attempts. A spell's *true* target was the exact center of an entire subject. *The center of everything is the doorway to success.* One had to first *connect* with the subject of their magic before they could direct it to a specific location therein. It was a lesson she'd promised to explore further in her journey of understanding and mastering the secrets of the magical arts.

Soon she was able to see the white target on the dummy's forehead clearly in her periphery. She gathered the Lightning

Course incantation in her mind and swiftly uttered it from her lips. The tips of her fingers tingled, and she extended both hands toward the center of the dummy. Purple light sparked from her palms, evolving into an electrifying glow that tinted the classroom a violet-blue hue.

She cupped her hands, forming the electricity into a ball. The air around her crackled and hissed, causing the tiny hairs on her forearms to stand on end. The ball intensified in power, tiny sparks escaping from between her fingers. Holding her ground, Perle launched the ball of lightning from her hands and toward her target.

The ball smashed into the dummy, jolting it backward in a perfect bobbing motion, its stability base preventing it from falling over completely. The lightning ball exploded in a shower of violet-blue sparks that encompassed the dummy, tiny streaks moving about its body like ants before fizzling out.

The tingling sensation from Perle's hands dissipated, and the magical surge in her body calmed. She exhaled.

Ms. Fitcher rose from her chair and approached the dummy. She studied it carefully, then circled around it, assessing it from top to bottom. Completing her circle, she ran her hand along the white target. Her eyebrows rose slightly, and then her face hardened. Finally, she scribbled something onto her clipboard.

"All right, Ms. Durand. You are finished. Return to your seat," Ms. Fitcher coolly instructed.

Noting the mistress's tone, Perle swallowed. *Did I pass?* Anxiety rose again in her chest. She was sure she hit the target straight on, but perhaps she was off by a few inches. Ms. Fitcher had eyes like a hawk, which didn't make this class any easier for Perle. As she slowly trudged back to her seat, she wondered how she had fared in her other classes.

She was skeptical about her prospects of passing her Herbology exam. She'd worked hard, trying to get on Professor Jericho's good side, but he remained as bitter as licorice. Even with all of Perle's merits, he was still tough on her, as he was with the other students. It wasn't uncommon for students to have to retake his class. Perle prayed to the stars that she didn't have to endure another year with Professor Jericho.

She couldn't believe her first semester at Once Upon Academy would be officially over in less than a week. Fortunately, she was scheduled to take all of her exams today, a small gift from the Headmistress, who had adjusted her schedule earlier in the year after Perle had saved the school from trouble. She looked forward to getting several days' head start on her winter break, indulging her parents on the many stories of her adventures at Once Upon Academy.

The bell rang, snapping Perle out of her thoughts. The other students got up around her and began heading to the exit. She quickly gathered her bag and followed the crowd. Ms. Fitcher stood by the door, handing out a small, rolled-up parchment tied with a red ribbon to each of the students as they exited. Some of them continued on without opening them, while others rolled them open on the spot.

Some jumped for joy, others wore long faces.

Taking her place at the back of the line, Perle watched each of the students' reactions. There was a balanced mix of sullen expressions and happy ones.

Great, she thought, raking her fingers nervously through her hair. There was no telling how hard Ms. Fitcher had been on the grading—this could go either way for her. She hated uncertainty. *I can't let everyone down.*

The last student glanced at his scroll, and trudged ahead with a blank expression on his face. Perle chewed her bottom lip. She was next.

Ms. Fitcher impassively looked down her nose at her, then held out a rolled-up scroll. "Like all things, Ms. Durand, there is always room for improvement."

Perle swallowed the lump forming in her throat. She moistened her lips. With a shaky hand, she slowly took the scroll "Did... Did I pass?" she asked meekly.

Ms. Fitcher grunted, brushed passed her, and returned to her desk. "Your assessment is there on your progress scroll. Off with you, now."

Perle opened her mouth to speak again, then closed it. She tightened her grip on the scroll, her eyes beginning to burn. There was no smile on Ms. Fitcher's face, no acknowledgement. Perle believed she did her very best, but unfortunately, it seemed it wasn't enough for Ms. Fitcher's high expectations. There was only one way to find out for certain.

Perle rushed back to her dorm, where she could check her final grade—and possibly cry afterwards—in private. She didn't expect to see her roommate Anala Firestar already there, hunched over the kitchen table. The beautiful dragon-shifter raked her fingers through her frazzled, red-orange hair as she stared sullenly at a piece of paper set in front of her.

As Perle closed the front door, Nuit rushed out of Perle's room, greeting her with happy meows and purrs. He wove back and forth between her ankles, and suddenly she felt calmer. Her little black cat's excitement filtered through her mind, but those feelings became bogged down with concern for her roommate, whose brown eyes glittered with tears. Emotions were running high everywhere it seemed; final exam season was definitely here in full force.

Perle stopped at the kitchen table. "Anala? Are you okay?"

Anala slowly looked up at her, then back to the paper and sighed. "I just... I can't... I don't know what to do. I'm in such a rut here. I can't believe it. For the first time, I'm stumped."

Perle cocked her head. "What's going on? Did you flunk one of your exams, too?"

Anala opened her mouth a moment, furrowed her brow, and then closed it. She gave Perle a quizzical look. "What? No. I can't decide what I'm going to do about this extra credit assignment for my Culinary class."

"What assignment?"

Anala pointed to the paper. "This is the specialty menu that will be served alongside the regular menu at the Winter Ball, and the Culinary students are allowed to choose what they would like to prepare."

A new wave of anxiety swallowed her mind, and Perle grimaced. The Winter Ball, one of Once Upon Academy's most prestigious events, was going to be held in five days, once classes had officially ended. The idea of experiencing her first ball was exciting, but after seeing how many of her peers had dates for the event, Perle had second thoughts. As admired as she was by her classmates for her heroic deeds, she'd never been asked to the ball, and she was too scared to do the asking.

Perle shut away those thoughts and glanced over the long list of dishes that spanned three columns. "There are lots of options. What's the problem?"

"What's the problem? Do you see all of these dishes? I can only choose *one* to prepare, and I have no idea which one to choose! I want to make the absolute perfect dish."

Perle smiled softly. "Why not choose the one that sounds the most appetizing to you?"

"That's the problem. They all sound appealing. I want to make them *all!*"

Perle looked at the list again. The menu items were a mix of various types of main courses, appetizers, desserts, drinks, and more, that were inspired by famous books and countries from around the world. "Well, it sounds like a great problem to have, if you ask me."

"No. It's not. If you were a culinary student, you would understand."

"Okay then. Since I've been your muse this school year, how about picking a

French dish?" Perle pointed out a few particular items on the list.

Anala grinned. "Hey, that's a good idea. All my French dishes helped me ace my classes, I should keep that momentum." She picked up a pencil and began circling all of the French dishes, one by one. Afterward, she handed the paper back to Perle. "Okay. Which one of these would you recommend?"

Perle raised her eyebrows and carefully reviewed the circled items. All of them sounded wonderful, but there was one in particular that caught her eye. Perle tapped the *Canelés de Bordeau* recipe and smiled. "*Celui-là.*"

Anala groaned. "Of course, you had to pick one of the most complicated ones."

"Maybe you'll get double extra credit for choosing a challenging recipe," Perle joked.

"Doubtful, but anything's possible, I guess. Anyway, it'll be fun trying something new."

"*Mon Papa* made them for my mother for her birthday once. They were divine."

"Lucky. Too bad I can't shadow him as his sous chef or something."

Perle laughed. "He's no professional chef. He just likes to spoil his wife and daughter."

"Thank you for saving me time and stress," Anala sighed with relief. "I get emotional about these sorts of things. A culinary chef always knows what they want to cook. It's in our blood. To not know what to make is just, well… a travesty."

Perle shrugged. "I guess I'm not much of a chef." She wondered if that was why her father was sometimes moody. Maybe it was more about him stressing out in the kitchen, and less about his inner beast being constantly agitated.

"That's okay. You're still my muse, at least," Anala said with an impish smile. "I'll have to research this recipe more." She tapped her chin in thought. "You wouldn't happen to have any advice on where to start, would you?"

Perle shrugged and shook her head at Anala's suggestion. "Sorry, I was never privy to Papa's recipes. I just know they were perfect. The crusts were caramelized, and the insides were deliciously soft, and melted on your tongue."

"Mmm. That sounds divine. I bet they will be a hit at the Winter Ball." Anala clapped her hands together excitedly.

Perle's anxious thoughts returned, and a bittersweet feeling filled her heart. With the ball fast approaching, she considered finding someone to ask as her date, but the looming thought of more rejection made her chicken out. Her thoughts traveled to Zeke Wolfson, one of the RAs, and a dear friend who helped her save the school from Tilda's destruction.

I wonder if he's going? She chewed her bottom lip.

Of all the people she'd met at OUA, she felt the most comfortable and safe around Zeke. He was a brooding, lone-wolf type, and his aggressive short temper was enough to scare off any potential date, but Perle saw a vulnerable side of him that he tended to keep hidden from others.

Beneath all that anger was an honorable man who was strong, protective, and dutiful. Zeke was also a busy man, however, not only being an RA, but also performing special tasks for the Headmistress. Perle had barely seen him for several weeks, and she wondered if he would even have time to go to the ball.

"Hey," Anala's voice returned Perle to the present. "Do you have a date yet?"

Perle frowned. *I wish she hadn't asked that.* "*Non*... I probably won't go."

Anala widened her eyes. "Not go? Are you crazy? The Winter Ball is one of OUA's premiere events. You *have* to go, especially for your first year. Besides, you'll miss my cooking."

"But I don't want to go alone," Perle said, her voice grim.

"You and me both, girl. I'm gonna find me an escort if it's the last thing I do."

Perle blinked. "You mean, you don't have anyone to go with, either?" She gawked at her roommate.

Anala was a dragon-shifter, and drop-dead gorgeous with long, fiery-red hair, creamy skin, and big brown eyes. She was built like a model, and there wasn't a dress in existence that could make her less than irresistible.

"Hey, I'm working on it," Anala said, shrugging. "It's hard, you know? I guess the fact that I'm a dragon intimidates them? I don't get it. I mean, it's not like I walk around shifted or something."

Perle gave her friend a reassuring pat on the back. "Well, I'm sure you'll have a better chance at finding a ball date than I will. You're more outgoing and social. I'm just a boring bookworm."

"Well, there's your problem," Anala said, rolling her eyes. "You're reading too much. You need to get out more. Or maybe just find yourself a fellow bookworm."

Perle half-smiled at the idea. "I'll think about it." Perle turned and headed for her room, Nuit happily trotting behind her.

"Whatever," Anala said. "I can't make you go, but all I'll say is that you'll be missing out on a once-in-a-lifetime opportunity."

"You can tell me all about it when it's over." Perle closed her bedroom door. She leaned her back against it and exhaled a deep sigh. *Great. Just one more thing to add to the end-of-the-year stress.*

She looked down at her scroll, which was now crinkled in the middle from her death-grip. *Guess it's time to face the facts.* She moved to the edge of her bed. Nuit hopped up and nestled next to her. He stared at the scroll curiously, then sniffed it.

"I just need to see it for closure," she projected telepathically to her familiar.

Nuit responded with a gentle, reassuring purr. Perle let out another sigh, and then unfurled the scroll. She grimly scanned the progress report.

Class Progress Report: Evocation
Accuracy: A+
First Attempt: A
Trajectory: A+
Focus: A
Posture: A
Incantation: A
Overall: A
Evocation I Final Grade: A+

Perle's mouth slowly dropped open, and she widened her eyes. *"Mon Dieu..."*

Perle read and re-read the progress report. *Is this a dream?* Maybe she'd received someone else's report. The look on Mistress Fitcher's face said all she needed to know when she handed Perle her scroll. But it wasn't a mistake; Perle's name was written clearly at the top of the report, and Mistress Fitcher's name was signed in elegant calligraphy at the bottom, along with a sparkling magical seal to confirm its authenticity.

Nuit meowed and stood up on his hind legs. She suddenly felt an overwhelming warmth and happiness in her mind.

"I passed... I passed? *I passed!*" She jumped off the bed and screamed, waving the paper in the air and dancing around her room.

Her burst of excitement startled Nuit, and he sought quick refuge under her bed. Anala suddenly barreled through Perle's door, her brown eyes glowing a deep-orange hue and her pupils becoming slitted, as though she were about to shift at any moment.

"Perle! Are you okay? What's going on? I heard a scream."

Perle beamed so wide, her cheeks hurt. She waved the parchment in front of Anala's face. "I passed my Evocation exam! Can you believe it?"

Anala swiped up the parchment, skimmed it, then grinned. "Hey, I knew you could do it. What was on this exam that stressed you out so much?"

"I couldn't even cast a single cantrip when I first got here. Now this? I just didn't think I would've progressed enough."

"You're the hardest working person I've ever met. You're always studying in the library or down in the practice chambers working on your next spell. In case you've forgotten, you're one of the heroes of OUA, so have a little more faith in yourself, girl." She handed the scroll back to Perle. "I'm going to be at the library for the rest of the day. Gotta get a head start on this recipe. The ball will be here before we know it."

After Anala left her room, Perle exhaled a deep sigh of relief. It was one less thing to worry about, but the Winter Ball continued to linger in her mind. *What am I going to do about that?*

She fell back on her bed with a soft bounce, splaying her arms and legs across the white-and-yellow floral sheets. She had enjoyed a few minutes of silence when she heard muffled knocks at the front door.

"Hey, Ben," Anala greeted.

Perle bolted up in bed. Ben Spriggan was another friend and fellow student who had helped her stop Tilda's madness. A student of Abjuration, Ben went above and beyond to help keep the peace at the school, becoming the eyes and ears for gossip and suspicious happenings that sometimes went unseen by the faculty and RAs. Ben also tended to be the bearer of bad news, and the fact that he was paying an unannounced visit didn't sit well with Perle.

"Sure. She's here. I'll grab her," Anala continued, then her muffled footsteps drew closer to Perle's room.

Perle opened her door before Anala could, looking toward Ben standing at the front door. He looked back at Perle, pale-faced, his short red hair frazzled. "*Bonjour,* Ben," she greeted, her tone slightly wary as she approached him.

Ben averted his gaze a moment and rubbed the back of his head. "Um…"

Uh oh. Is he hearing more sounds in the basement again? Another fire beetle in the

46

library? The harrowing scenarios flooded Perle's mind. "Is everything okay?" she asked, tilting her head.

Ben took a deep breath and shook his head solemnly. "It's Zeke. He's..."

She perked up at the mention of Zeke, and her heart gave a small thump. "What did he do this time?"

He steadied his gaze on hers. "He's in the infirmary..."

Concern flooded her heart. "What happened? Did he get into another fight?"

"I don't know. He's been in a coma all morning and hasn't woken up."

Her mouth dropped open. "Oh no..."

Nuit let out a long, drawn-out yowl, echoing her sentiment.

"Zeke?" Anala broke in. "I swear, that wolf gets into more trouble than anyone I know." She gently nudged Perle. "I'm sure he'll be okay. We shifters are a tough bunch."

Perle frowned. *Maybe she's right, but I have to know for certain.*

"I'll take you to him. Come on," Ben said, beckoning Perle with a wave of his hand.

"Keep me posted," Anala said. She headed down the hallway toward the library.

Perle and Ben rushed across campus toward the infirmary. Nuit scurried alongside them, sending calming, reassuring vibes to her distressed mind, but as much as her familiar tried, it didn't calm the intense beating of her heart.

CHAPTER 3

ZEKE OPENED HIS EYES TO a dark and hazy world. This didn't appear to be Once Upon Academy, but something about this strange place felt familiar. *Where am I? Or is it another nightmare?* His head throbbed. Sitting up, he tried to remember the last thing that happened, but everything was a blur.

His ears perked up at a faint, distant sound. A shapely, feminine silhouette appeared ahead of him in the distance. Zeke sniffed once and narrowed his eyes, trying to discern the identity of stranger outlined in the grey haze. The scent was familiar—recent. As the figure neared, his suspicions were soon confirmed.

The woman, tall, lithe, and wearing a long black dress that hugged every curve, stopped before him. His mind suddenly became clear. *No... It can't be...*

The woman smirked with lips painted the blackest of night, contrasting sharply with her fair skin. Her entrancing brown eyes glittered with amusement. "So... we meet again, pup."

Zeke's eyes widened. It *was* her. That evil witch Tilda who hurt him and his friends and nearly destroyed Once Upon Academy. But what was she doing here? Or had she dragged him into her evil world? Perhaps he was dead, and this was the nightmare that he would forever endure.

Zeke growled and tried to stand, but a searing pain shot through his body like an electric shock. His knees buckled. Cringing, he collapsed back to the ground.

"You really shouldn't do that," Tilda mocked. "And to think, you and your annoying little friends thought you could get rid of me so easily. As I said before, this isn't over."

"I don't believe you, witch," Zeke said through clenched teeth.

Tilda knelt before him and gently raised his chin with her slender fingers. "Believe what you want. You are mine, now. Foolish pup." Her eyes narrowed. "And *she* thought she could uncover my secrets. But instead, she unleashed one of my curses. And what luck? You just happened to be the lucky candidate. Though, I would've preferred the Headmistress, instead. But you will do just fine." She paused, and her lips turned in a devious smirk. "Ah, and what a wonderful accident, it is. I will have to personally thank that naïve Headmistress and her minions for helping me. I'm rather amused about the irony. Let's see how events unfold, shall we?"

Zeke wrinkled his nose. "What curse?"

Tilda laughed. "Oh, I can't spoil the surprise. But your dear little Perle will be in for quite a shock when she sees you again. What a fitting end for Beau's beloved daughter." She cackled darkly, then turned and walked away.

Zeke blinked. Tilda's image blurred, and the world around him began darkening again. "Wait! What are you talking about? What does Perle have to do with this? Get back here now!"

Tilda continued walking without didn't respond.

He tried to focus on shifting form, but something about this world prevented his powers from manifesting. Tilda's image disappeared in the haze. The air grew thinner, and it was becoming harder to breathe. He panicked, his protective wolf instincts urging him to shift, but something about this place prevented him from using his ability. He clenched his chest with a shaky hand, and finally, he conceded. Everything around him went dark.

Zeke awoke with a start and let out a terrified gasp, as if he had been held underwater for too long.

"Zeke!" a female voice called.

His heart was pounding as pain, fear, and panic gripped his bones. Instinctively, he attempted to shift, but his mind was too scattered, he couldn't concentrate. *Is this the curse I'm feeling?*

"Zeke! Are you okay?" the female voice called again, now becoming distinctive in his mind.

Zeke turned to its source. Bright lights filled his vision, and the sounds of low hums steadily pulsated in his ears. He squinted, adjusting his eyes to the light. Inhaling deeply, he caught a whiff of medicinal herbs, fresh bandages, and something much more pleasant. His vision focused, and he saw Perle and Ben standing over his bedside. Perle's black cat, Nuit sat nearby, giving itself a bath. Zeke's gaze settled on Perle, the alluring, sweet scent of her grape perfume calming his mind.

"Perle?" he called in a low volume, his voice cracking. "Is that…"

Perle's bronze face brightened. "*Oui!* It's me! And Ben. What happened? Why are you here?"

So many questions. Even Zeke didn't know entirely what had happened. However, even as they talked, he began to feel more like himself, and he was grateful that fast healing was one of the benefits of his shifter powers.

"I don't know why I'm here," Zeke finally said as he struggled to sit up in bed. He rubbed his temples, trying to remember. Thankfully, his head no longer ached. He assessed his surroundings. He was back at Once Upon Academy, in a private room of the infirmary. He was no stranger to this dreaded place. He'd come here enough times that the nurses had given him his own designated bed.

"Hey, Zeke. Take it easy," Ben said.

Zeke grunted. "I'm fine. I heal fast."

"Yeah, but you obviously didn't heal fast enough because you are here," Perle retorted. "Do you remember anything at all?"

Zeke slowly shook his head.

Nurse Berri approached his bed. The deeply troubled look on the blue faerie's round face indicated the severity of Zeke's condition. "Oh, thank the stars you've finally awakened."

Zeke furrowed his brow. "How long was I out?"

"Since this morning. You weren't moving, and a few of us were beginning to assume the worst. I'm glad we were wrong."

"What happened to me?" Zeke asked.

Berri pursed her thin, sapphire-colored lips. She approached Zeke's bedside table, where numerous magical healing devices sat. She placed her hands over a green, glowing orb that hovered a few inches above the table—meant to continuously provide healing energy to the patient—and closed her eyes. Moments later, her hands emitted a similar greenish glow. The magic transferred into the orb, causing it to grow brighter and amplify in power.

Berri opened her eyes. "You were struck with dark magic. The staff has been investigating its source for some time now. You have been placed under strict observation until this matter has been settled." Her gaze hardened. "I fear it might be some kind of curse."

A curse... Zeke swallowed, and thought about his conversation with Tilda. *Was that a dream?*

Perle gaped. "What do you mean 'a curse'?"

Berri nodded solemnly. "There are many curses that cannot be detected by conventional magic."

"Isn't there a way to get rid of it?" Ben asked.

"There is, but..." Berri sighed. "The problem is determining the curse's type. None of us will know until it manifests. And who knows when that will happen? If it ever does happen?"

Zeke blinked. "'If? You mean I could be stuck with this curse for the rest of my life and may never know what it is?"

"It's possible..." Berri responded in a meek tone.

Zeke growled. "Well, there's no way I'm letting that happen. I'll make this curse manifest if it's the last thing I do."

"You can't force its manifestation. It will reveal itself on its own," Berri explained. "But I must caution you that we do not know what sort of curse this is. It could be deadly for all we know. We must not rush this manifestation, if we can learn more about it."

"How can this be studied? And how will I know when the curse manifests?"

Berri pinned her gaze on him. "You'll know." She left his bedside. "I must tend to the other patients. Please remain in bed for at least one more night for further observation."

Zeke fisted the white sheets. "I've been here long enough. I still have work to do around here."

"The Headmistress has relieved you of your RA duties until further notice."

Zeke sneered. The thought of the Headmistress not needing him agitated his wolf. *Does she think I'm too weak to do my duties?* "I feel fine. I'm ready to work again," he insisted, then began to slide out of bed. He wore nothing but a thin, turquoise-colored medical gown, which was emblazoned with OUA's emblem over his heart. Placing his bare feet on the cold floor, he shivered a moment, then slowly stood up. His legs were weak, but at least he could stand on his own.

"Zeke, please, don't..." Perle pleaded, reaching out for him.

Zeke slapped her hand away. "I told you I'm fine."

Perle's eyes dulled. Her gaze flitted to the floor and she held her rejected hand. "She's just trying to take care of you."

Zeke watched Perle a moment and swallowed a lump in his throat. He sensed the dejection in her voice, her eyes. Perhaps he was too harsh, but his mind was a mess right now.

Berri hustled back to him, then stopped in her tracks when he glowered at her.

"C'mon, Zeke," Ben said. "Berri's the nurse. She knows what's best for you."

"*I* know what's best for me, Spriggan." Zeke glared at Ben, then returned his attention to Berri. "You can't force me to stay here."

Berri sighed. "No, Mr. Wolfson, I cannot. The Headmistress did not give that order. Perhaps she knows you too well." Without another word, she spun back around and began heading to another bedridden patient across the partitioned room.

Zeke smiled slightly to himself. Perhaps the Headmistress *had* known him that well. He cast a cool gaze at Perle and Ben, and then slowly began making his way to the infirmary's exit. "I'm outta here."

He had reached the exit when Ben suddenly came up from behind him and blocked the doorway.

"Wait," Ben said.

Zeke let out a low, throaty growl. He and Ben had gone through some adventures together, most notably when they'd joined forces with Perle and stopped Tilda the first time. Though Zeke and Ben had made amends, he still wasn't fond of the Abjuration student. Besides, Zeke was certain Ben and Perle had grown close. Zeke was always working, and rarely had the time or desire for anything else. He loved to stay busy, but it didn't come without its consequences.

Perle joined Ben at the doorway, creating a double barrier. Zeke frowned at the both of them. They probably saw each other every day. Envy tugged at his mind. He'd do anything to trade places with Ben, but he had his duties. Zeke cared for Perle, perhaps more than he should, but at least he could be assured that she would be okay—even if she was hanging around a goofy trickster like Ben.

Zeke finally shouldered past his friends. "For the last time, I'm fine," he muttered, heading down the long hallway.

"Yes, but..." Perle began. She sank her teeth into her bottom lip. "Are you sure? I mean, there's a lot going on around here, being near the end of the school year and all. I just... I don't want anything else to happen to you."

Zeke stopped walking. He felt his throat tighten as he noted the genuine concern in her soft voice. There was so much he wished he could say to her, but he didn't know how to form his feelings into cohesive words. Emotions were not something he knew how to express clearly, thanks to the many years of pain he'd endured at home. His father had once said, "the heart is a weapon. It can form the greatest allies, or the deadliest of enemies. Emotions are a byproduct of the heart. Succumb to emotions, and you are already dead." Zeke tried every day to live by those words. But the more he tried, the harder the emotions came, especially while he was around Perle. His struggle to find balance within himself seemed never ending.

Zeke looked over his shoulder at her. "I'm just glad it's almost over. I'm ready for a break."

She smiled wistfully. "Are you going home?"

Home. Zeke wrinkled his nose. Just the word alone was triggering. His family rejected him for being too weak and unable to control his powers. He'd since been on a quest to earn their respect once and for all. Being a son of the notorious Big Bad Wolf, his odds in life were already stacked against him. Being feared and rejected by both his family and peers for his bloodline brought him nothing but emotional pain. Zeke had hoped his time spent at Once Upon Academy would help him learn how to be accepted, by himself and others.

Zeke shook his head at Perle. "I don't know... Probably not," he finally replied. "I'd rather stick around here to help the janitors clean the school. Or maybe I'll help the event committee decorate for the Winter Ball." *Winter Ball...* He mentally swore as the words flung from his mouth. He wasn't sure what he was dreading most: the mere thought of the ball or going home. Though he owned exactly one formal suit, he'd never attended any balls before, nor did he intend to start. It was bad enough he was urged by the Headmistress to go to the celebration dinner last semester for helping to save the school. While the food had been great, parties just weren't his thing. Contrary to his shifter species, he was definitely not social.

Perle's face lit up in a mix of confusion and surprise. "Oh, the Winter Ball. About that..."

Zeke shrugged. He assumed she was already going with someone—probably Ben. "I'm not going."

"Y-You're not? Why?"

"I don't have time to go to some stupid ball. But you and Ben have fun."

Perle and Ben exchanged glances and blushed.

Ben scratched the back of his head and looked sheepishly back at Zeke. "Uh, actually, there's already someone I'm planning on asking."

"Whatever," Zeke said, continuing down the hallway.

Despite Zeke's insistence on being alone, Perle and Ben followed him back to his dorm. Finally, as Zeke placed his hand on the door handle, he turned back to his friends. "Look, you two don't have to keep babysitting me."

Perle frowned. "I can't help but wonder if all this happened while you were performing a job for the Headmistress. If so, why would she put you in danger?"

Zeke ground his teeth. "I wasn't doing a job for her. At least, I don't think I was. Besides, she would never put me in danger. Of that, I'm certain."

"Then how could you have gotten this curse?" Perle held up her hands.

"I don't know, but I'm going to find out."

"Maybe we can all help," Ben suggested.

"No. The curse is in me, so it's my problem," Zeke retorted.

Perle's lips formed a thin line. "No one deserves to live like that."

Zeke clenched his jaw. *She has no idea. My whole life is a curse.* Being a son of the Big Bad Wolf was already a curse in itself, and the endless rejection that came with it. "It's who I am, and I've come to accept it. I'll fix my own problems. Stay out of it," he ordered.

Perle lowered her head. "I'm sorry..."

With a grunt, he spun and unlocked the door. The pain in Perle's voice made him cringe internally with guilt. He sighed. "Don't be sorry," he said in a regretful tone. He wished she didn't care for him so much. He was trouble, after all. The last thing he wanted was for her life to be in danger because of him. It was up to him to protect her from this curse—to protect her from himself.

CHAPTER 4

THE TROUBLING EVENTS THAT unfolded two days ago became a blur in Perle's mind as she traveled in an elegant, white, magical pumpkin carriage back to her French homeland. With all of her exams done—and passed—she had several days' head start on her winter break. After bidding farewell to Ben and Anala, she eagerly packed her bags and prepared for the journey home. Perle hadn't seen Zeke since the infirmary, and it troubled her to think that he might have been deliberately avoiding her. She wondered how he was faring. His problem was unfortunately out of her hands, and he seemed adamant about keeping it that way. At this point, all she could do was pray to the stars that he would be okay.

Her worries were soon pushed aside when she noticed the familiar rolling hills and grape vineyards that dotted Riquewihr's countryside. She beamed. *I'm home.*

The carriage, shrouded under a veil of illusion magic that made it invisible to the locals, traveled along the shoulder of the narrow road, away from the local traffic. The ride was surprisingly smooth, a spell was most likely put in place to ensure that. Once Upon Academy's actual location was unknown, so magic was the only way to transport the students to and from the school.

Perle lovingly stroked Nuit, who was curled in her lap, purring contentedly. Staring out the carriage window at the passing landscape, Perle sensed something different. Everything around her appeared the same, and yet, *she* felt different. When she had left here five months ago, she was inexperienced and doubtful. Now, she was back, more determined, and with a deeper understanding of herself. She'd never thought that Once Upon Academy would have been able to work such a miracle on her.

"We're here, Ms. Durand," the carriage driver announced.

Perle's smile grew, spotting her village coming into view just ahead.

The carriage stopped in front of a quaint, 18ᵗʰ century-style cottage, with its exposed timbers and whitewashed stonework. Beds of roses decorated the front. Her parents, Beau and Jolie stood outside, smiling and waving to the carriage.

Perle's smile turned lopsided. *So much for surprising them. Oh, well. It's still good to see them.* Not waiting for the driver, she flung open the door, jumped out of the carriage, and rushed into her parents' arms with a tight embrace. Nuit followed, meowing happily, echoing her sentiments.

"*Maman! Papa!* I am so happy to see you both again!" Perle exclaimed.

Her father, Beau, kissed the top of her head, then pulled back from the embrace. He gently squeezed her shoulders, assessing her from head to toe with his grey-colored eyes, and beamed. He stood over six feet tall, his height and strong build easily dwarfing Perle and Jolie.

"Welcome back, *ma chérie fille.*"

Jolie kissed her cheek. "We've missed you," she said, her dark-brown eyes glittering with happy tears. Jolie's height only reached the middle of Beau's chest. She was thin and lithe with ageless bronze skin and soft, curly brown hair.

"I've missed you, too!" Perle said. "How did you know I was coming today?"

"Fairy Godmother sent us a message yesterday." Beau replied.

"Ah…" Perle chewed her bottom lip. Her nervous heart skipped a beat. "W-What else did she say?" Perle had requested that the Headmistress not inform her parents about Tilda. The last thing she wanted was for her parents to worry. Whether or not the Headmistress had respected her wishes had yet to be seen.

"Other than you were arriving early? Nothing more," Jolie said.

Perle nodded and exhaled a small sigh of relief.

The driver unloaded Perle's luggage and returned to the carriage. He waved goodbye to Perle and her family and took off down the road again. The sunlight reflected off the carriage like a glittering curtain, and then suddenly the carriage disappeared.

"Well, now." Beau began, gathering the luggage. "I'm sure you have lots of stories to share." With the bags in tow, he headed for the front door.

"I do, but first, *j'ai faim!*" Perle rubbed her growling belly. She sniffed, detecting a familiar mouthwatering aroma wafting in the air as Beau opened the door. "Is that—"

"Ratatouille?" Beau looked back at her and grinned. "*Oui,* and there are some other surprises for you, too." He went inside.

Jolie walked with Perle. "He was up all night cooking. I don't think he got any sleep." Jolie chuckled.

Perle cringed. "Oh, I wish he hadn't done that."

Jolie shook her head. "You know you can't stop your father once he puts his mind to something."

As Perle entered the cottage, she was consumed with pleasant memories of her childhood. She'd only been gone for five months, but it felt so much longer. She stared at the common room. She'd grown up in this house, and yet everything around the house looked different. The coffee table she used to hide under when she was five looked tiny—in fact, the entire room looked smaller than she remembered. Things that used to look bigger to her had become smaller as she grew, but it wasn't until now, after leaving the house completely, that she realized just how big and small things really were.

"Are you alright?" Jolie asked, snapping Perle out of her thoughts.

Perle looked at her mother, who regarded her with a slight crease in her brow. "*Oui*, I just... missed home a lot."

Jolie smiled reassuringly. "We did, too, our first year. Then, as the semesters went by, the academy felt more like a home away from home."

The academy had started to feel that way toward the end. She'd made friends, and spent almost every waking moment at her happy place, the place that reminded her the most of home, the library.

Perle visited all of the rooms in the house—including her own—familiarizing herself with her past again, before joining her parents in the kitchen where a massive spread was waiting for her. Perle gawked at the smorgasbord of some of her favorite dishes—beef bourguignon, *gratin dauphinoise*, quiche, *gougeres*, and of course, ratatouille. Another section of the table was full of desserts like *palmiers*, poached pears, *canelés*, honey-glazed pear tarts, cherry *clafoutis*, and chocolate mousse. In the middle of the table sat a bottle of homemade white wine.

Perle scanned all the food again, and her mouth dropped open. *Je suis au paradis! This is unbelievable!* "Papa! I can't possibly eat all of this."

Nuit rushed under the table and greedily tore into a bowl of chopped raw salmon.

Seated at the head of the table, Beau rubbed his hands together, grinning at his creations. "Don't worry, *fille*. It will not go to waste," he said with a wink.

Jolie rolled her eyes and laughed. "Unfortunately, that beastly appetite didn't disappear with the rest of that curse."

Perle's smile faltered as her mind briefly revisited past events. Sighing, she pushed those thoughts aside, and took a seat at the table, across from her mother. She picked up an empty bowl and scanned the overwhelming selection of food, unsure of where to begin. At that moment, she thought about Anala and her troubles.

This must be how she was feeling. If she saw all this, she'd probably faint. Finally, Perle settled on the dish closest to her—the ratatouille—and spooned out a hefty portion into her bowl.

"So, I gave you the food," Beau said, once they all began eating. "Now it's your turn to give me some stories. I know you have plenty of them. And don't spare the details."

Perle swallowed a portion of her stew. It was divine as always. She looked at her father with slight surprise and relief. *So, Ms. Fay hadn't told them after all. The Headmistress really* did *keep her promise.* "Well..." Perle began.

"Beau." Jolie shot him a hard stare. "She's barely been back an hour. Give the poor girl some time to relax first."

"Bah." He flicked his hand dismissively. "There's always time for stories. Especially from Once Upon Academy. She might have a story about one of her favorite classes or teachers. Or, you know, she might have met someone, and—"

"Aha!" Jolie lifted her chin and pinned him with an accusing gaze. "I thought we'd agreed not to prod into her personal life?"

Blushing, Perle averted her gaze and dipped her spoon in the stew. "It's all right, Mother. I haven't met anyone yet."

Beau popped two *gourgers* in his mouth, and then froze, his cheeks bulging and his eyes wide with shock. "You haven't?" he mumbled with his mouth full.

"Beau!" Jolie grimaced.

He swallowed the cheese bites. "The Winter Ball is in three days. Do you have an escort at least?"

Sighing, Perle idly stirred her stew. "No, Papa. I guess everyone else had other plans. I'll just have to go by myself."

He scowled. "Going alone? To a *ball*? Nonsense!" He put his hands on the table and balled them into fists.

"Beau…" Jolie said softly.

"No, Jolie. I cannot and will not allow our *belle fille* to go to an exquisite ball alone."

75

"It's all right, Papa," Perle assured. "I... I'm not upset." She forced a small smile. "I'll make sure I have fun."

He looked at Perle for several moments, then sighed. "I only want the best for you, *fille*."

"I know." Perle's smile wavered the more she thought about the ball. *So what if I do go alone? I won't let that stop me from enjoying my time at the Winter Ball.* She continued eating, the deliciousness of the food helping her block out her sadness and doubts.

Perle changed the subject and indulged her parents on stories about her exploration around the academy, her classes, and her new friends. She was careful not to mention Tilda. Though the evil woman was gone, Perle knew that wouldn't stop her father from worrying every second.

Perle mentioned the grand library, which got her mother's full attention. Perle hadn't read anywhere near the amount of books her mother had read, but the library had become Perle's sanctuary, just as it was Jolie's.

An hour passed, and Perle was exhausted and dry-mouthed from all of her storytelling. All the food was completely devoured, thanks to Beau, but Perle got a chance to taste some of everything, and it reminded her how much she truly had missed home. The three of them relaxed around the kitchen table, enjoying a glass of aged, homemade red wine as an after-dinner refresher.

"You're certainly not the same girl that left here five months ago," Jolie said, her expression softening. "There's a different glow about you. You've matured with your magic."

Perle's smile returned a little stronger. "I have learned so much in such a short time at the academy. I feel so much more in control of my powers."

"I had no doubt about your ability," Jolie said. "Magic runs in your veins."

"I guess this means we can put all the electronics back in your room, now, eh?" Beau laughed.

Perle chuckled, thinking about all the appliances, phones, and other electronic devices she'd inadvertently destroyed in the past. "I suppose." Nuit brushed his body against Perle's legs, and she felt the cat project some nervous vibes in her mind. Her smile broadened in amusement. "Nuit isn't so sure, though."

"Hm?" Beau furrowed his brow and peered under the table.

"He is my familiar," Perle explained. Noticing the curious looks on her parents' faces, she exhaled a deep sigh and prepared to indulge them in another long story. Like the others, she didn't spare the details, but was careful to not mention Tilda.

Nuit jumped in Perle's lap and peered over the table at Beau and Jolie.

"Familiars are an odd phenomenon," Jolie said when Perle finished her story. She picked up her wine glass and casually swirled its contents.

Perle regarded her parents curiously. "I don't understand why neither of you possessed familiars."

Jolie raised her eyebrows. "Why would you think that?"

Perle shrugged. "Familiars tend to be attracted to magic, so I thought that since you and Papa possess magic, acquiring a familiar would come easy."

"Nothing comes easy when it comes to magic, *fille*. Familiars are special creatures that share an inseparable bond with their masters. It was just not meant to be for us to possess ones of our own. But that's okay. The lack of a familiar does not make someone more or less magically inclined. The threads of magic span a wide spectrum of abilities. Besides..." She smiled coyly. "I'd pity the poor familiar who'd end up with someone like your father for a master."

Beau stopped in mid-sip of his wine. "Hey! I would make a great master."

Jolie rolled her eyes. "Not with that short temper of yours."

He pouted.

Perle laughed. "Oh, you two."

"Anyway," Jolie continued, "I'm glad to see you've discovered this special aspect of your magical abilities. You blossomed late, and I knew a place like Once Upon Academy would be perfect for you."

"It's been a learning experience, that's for sure," Perle said. "I've never been more grateful to have Nuit at my side. I mean, he's saved my life, and—"

"Saved your life?" Beau perked up, setting down his glass with a light clink.

Uh oh. Perle hesitated. She tried to fish for the right words to move the conversation elsewhere, but her mind was flustered from shock. "Um..." She nervously spun her finger around the rim of her empty wine glass.

A small crease appeared at Jolie's brow. "What happened?"

I guess there's no running from this now. Perle exhaled a deep sigh, and told them the story of Tilda.

Beau slammed his fist on the table, causing the empty dishes and glasses to vibrate and clink noisily. He gritted his teeth. "She... That... that witch! I can't believe no one from the academy informed us!"

Perle shook her head. "I asked the Headmistress to not inform you about it."

"W-Why would you do that?" Jolie's eyes became glassy.

"Because I didn't want you two to worry. Especially you, Papa." Perle glanced warily at Beau.

Beau growled. "Worried? I'm *furious* that witch returned! She almost killed you!"

"Please, Papa. We managed to stop her. She's trapped in her twisted world and unable to escape. She's gone from here, I promise. The rune book was confiscated by the school. The Headmistress has everything under control."

Jolie's lips thinned. "Please understand, *fille*. We worry because we love you very much."

Perle nodded. "I understand. And I love you, too."

Beau's dissatisfied frown remained. "She may be gone, but I still don't like it. You said you got that book from her, right? She was posing as a librarian here in town? What if she gave out more of those dreaded rune books to other people?" He sprang up from his chair. "I should go into town and look around for more of Tilda's books. I won't let her hurt anyone else."

"Sit down, Beau," Jolie said. "You're overreacting again. Tilda is no longer a threat, according to Perle's story. Now, I think we should all focus on something more pleasant—like the upcoming Winter Ball."

Perle was relieved to move on from the subject of Tilda, but returning the conversation to the Winter Ball only brought back her anxiety. "I told you I was going. What else is there to talk about?" she asked with a light shrug.

Jolie beamed. "You need a fantastic gown, of course! And I know just the place in town to get one." She raised her eyebrows at Beau, who appeared deep in thought. "That is, if your father doesn't object."

Perle perked up a little and looked to her father hopefully. She knew how much he adored dress shopping for his wife and daughter, spoiling them to no end with tailor-made gowns that would make a queen jealous. But he still seemed to be in a bitter mood about Tilda, and dress shopping was probably the last thing on his mind.

"Huh? Yeah, sure. Fine," Beau said absently, his frown still present.

Jolie gave Perle a wink. "Excellent. Tomorrow, you and I will take a trip to the store and get you a gown that will guarantee to turn heads. You won't be alone at the ball for long, that's for sure."

Perle beamed with excitement. It wasn't often she and her mother went on shopping trips together. It would be nice to spend a girls' day out, enjoying each other's company and talking about books.

Perle looked back at her father, and her heart stuttered. His troubled expression indicated that Tilda was still on his mind, and he wouldn't stop thinking about it until he had closure—whatever that might be. *Perhaps tomorrow when I return with my new gown, he will forget all about Tilda,* Perle thought.

She could only hope.

CHAPTER 5

PERLE HAD A GOOD NIGHT'S sleep despite the troubling talk she had with her parents yesterday about Tilda. She didn't know why that woman continued to haunt her after Perle and her friends had defeated her. The matter was now in the hands of the Headmistress, anyway. But somehow, Perle couldn't shake off the feeling that something was still wrong. Something beyond Tilda. Of course—*Zeke*. He was all alone somewhere dealing with a curse. Her heart ached for him.

"I was thinking, you might look good in yellow," Jolie said.

Perle blinked and stared out the passenger's window of her mother's tiny car at the passing landscape. Then she looked at her mother. "Huh?"

"Are you listening?" Jolie smiled. "Or are you thinking about your father's troubles again?"

"Maybe..."

"Well stop. He's just being protective of his family. It's his inner beast kicking in again. It never went away even after his curse got lifted. Though, I can't help but be grateful for his genuine concern for the people he loves."

Perle's face softened. Her parents had the perfect storybook relationship, and they were truly living their happily ever after. Her thoughts wandered back to Zeke, who was apparently still angry with the world.

"Mother, how did you manage to get Papa to open up?"

"Eh?" Jolie raised an eyebrow.

Perle explained to her about Zeke and his troubles. Somehow, talking about this to her mother eased a little pain from Perle's heart.

Jolie grinned when she finished. "So, you *do* have someone of interest, hmm?"

Blushing, Perle fidgeted with her hands. "It's not like that. Zeke is a friend. He's not really a relationship kind of person."

Jolie snorted. "Trust me, I thought that about your father, too, when we first met. It seems to run in the family that we tend to be attracted to the stubborn ones. But the challenge and struggle is what adds to the excitement of falling in love, no?

"If you really care about this young man, then be there for him. Let him know how you feel. He may try to push you away, but don't give up. Show him compassion. Who knows if he's ever gotten any love from his family?"

Perle frowned. "I don't know what his family situation is like. He doesn't talk much about them."

"Well, don't prod. He'll open up someday. Maybe. Your father did."

Perle nodded. "I think I'll go back to the school a few days early, before the ball starts. Zeke mentioned he was going to help clean up the school and set up for the event."

"That's a great idea," Jolie said. "Who knows? Maybe this might be the year Zeke decides to attend the ball, especially after he sees you in the dress we find." She winked.

"Doubtful. Zeke isn't the social gathering type."

"I never thought your father was, either, but he was just full of surprises. We were show-stoppers at the ball, let me tell you. He's quite the dancer, if you can believe it. Now, about that dress... " Jolie stopped the car.

They had arrived in Colmar, a small town twenty minutes south from their home. They were parked along the curb in front of a small boutique shop in the heart of the town's shopping district.

Perle spotted a fanciful, off-the-shoulder gown displayed in the window. The dress sparkled in a golden gradient, like bright stars against a sunset sky. The colors reminded her of Zeke's intriguing eyes, and the mysterious wolf that possessed him. She beamed. "I agree, Mother. Yellow would be perfect."

Perle awoke the next morning to the sounds of her parents' arguing voices rising from the kitchen. She sat up in bed. Nuit meowed from her bedside, staring up at her intently. A feeling of concern was projected into her mind, and she frowned at her familiar.

"What's going on?"

He meowed again, and then padded out of her bedroom.

"No, this is *not* over!" her father's angry voice boomed.

Perle jumped out of bed and rushed through her bedroom door. Her parents were in the kitchen, facing each other in an angry stare-down. It was one of the rare times in her life Perle had witnessed her parents in such a strong disagreement.

"You're being too relaxed about this!" Beau growled. "Tilda could be out there at this very moment using her dark magic to hurt others just to get to me. She must be stopped!"

"You are being irrational!" Jolie snapped back, crossing her arms. "I spoke with Fairy Godmother, as well as the Headmistress about it, and they assured me that Tilda is gone. They have been working tirelessly to secure the school in time for the Winter Ball.

Beau's eyes went wide. "When did you talk to them?"

"Last night when you were asleep, because I knew you would act like this."

"Act like what?"

Perle cleared her throat. Her parents paused and looked her way. Perle frowned at them and leaned against the door frame. "I should've never said anything," she muttered.

Jolie uncrossed her arms. "No, *fille*. I am glad you told us. Your father is just being unreasonable again." Jolie pinned him with a stern gaze.

His jaw clenched. "I am *not* being unreasonable. Tilda is dangerous, don't you see?"

"And what do *you* expect to do?" Jolie asked. "The situation is under control. Reel in that anger, Beau. She is not a threat to any of us."

"Papa..." Perle pushed off the doorframe and approached him. "You can't keep letting the past control you. Tilda isn't even here, and she's still haunting you." As she said that, however, a thought niggled in the back of her mind. *Tilda was contained, but what if she finds a way to escape?* Perle couldn't bear to witness Tilda tormenting her parents again. Maybe it was just her father's concern, but she had to know for certain that Tilda was truly stopped.

He tensed a moment, then relaxed his broad shoulders and sighed. "I care about you both too much to let someone like Tilda harm you."

"If anything, I think our daughter has proven to everyone that she can hold her own," Jolie said. "You need to believe in her. And she's right, you know. The more you worry about Tilda, the more power she has over you."

Beau clenched and unclenched his fists, then slumped down in a chair at the kitchen table. He sighed deeply, running his hands through his dark-brown hair. "I… I suppose you're right…"

Jolie's face softened. "Of course, I'm right." She gently placed her hand on his shoulder. "Now, I think we need to spend as much time as we can with our daughter before she returns to the school for the Winter Ball."

Beau suddenly perked up, his anger ebbing like an ocean's tide. "The ball…?

The ball!" He sprang back out of his chair and spun to Perle. "Did you get your gown already?"

Perle grinned, relieved to see her father in high spirits again. "I did, Papa. Do you want to see?"

"Wait... You mean, you got a dress and didn't show me?"

"We shopped yesterday while you were busy sulking," Jolie said simply.

Beau huffed. "I hope you went to Candlewick's Boutique."

Jolie gawked. *"Vous plaisantez!* That place is all the way in Paris! No, Beau, we did not take a four-hour trip to Candlewick's. Instead, we went to the next best place." She nodded to Perle.

Smiling, Perle rushed back to her bedroom and retrieved the ball gown hanging in her closet. Her heart swelled at the beautiful golden gown. She couldn't wait to wear it at the ball.

As soon as she returned to the kitchen, Beau's eyes widened, and his face paled.

Perle spun around, holding the dress in front of her. "Isn't it wonderful, Papa? And it's my favorite shade of yellow."

Beau's mouth opened, then he closed it. His stare hardened and he turned to Jolie. "How could you?"

Jolie rolled her eyes. "It would take weeks—possibly months—to get a custom-tailored dress from Candlewick's. And who knows how many other orders they're probably swamped with at this time? We can't risk it, Beau."

"Like the stars, we won't!" Beau growled. He pointed at Perle. "No daughter of mine is wearing that dress."

Perle blinked. "What's wrong with this dress? I like it very much."

"Do you really like it, or do you only like it because that was the only yellow dress the store had?"

"I really like it." Perle blinked. "Wait. How did you know it was the only yellow dress in stock?"

"I had a hunch. What? You don't think I know anything about my own daughter?

About how every specific thread, seam, and fabric needs to lay so that the light hits the dress's colors properly in order to complement your skin tone? About how the material's quality needs to be both soft and comfortable, yet durable?

"No, but..." She looked at her dress again. "I like this dress. I really do. And not because it was the only yellow one, either."

"So if it were a blue dress in that exact style, would you have still picked it up?" Beau lifted an eyebrow.

"Um... Probably not..."

Beau nodded curtly. "I rest my case."

Perle sighed. His stubbornness made her head hurt.

Jolie narrowed her eyes at him. "Just because you got my dress from Candlewick's doesn't mean she wants one from there, too. Besides, she said she liked that dress. There's no time to get a tailor-made one."

Beau shook his head. "He'll make time. The owner has known me long enough.

He owes me a favor, anyway." He stormed out of the kitchen and looked over his shoulder. "Get dressed, *fille*. We're going to Paris."

CHAPTER 6

ZEKE WATCHED THE MAGICAL pumpkin carriage make its way down the rocky mountain path until it finally disappeared in a white cloud of snow flurries. He slung his duffel bag over his shoulder, gazed further up the path, and sighed. With the Headmistress's encouragement and insistence, Zeke decided to return home and face what he feared most—his past.

He was more than content and willing to remain at the school. He could have helped the cleaning crew and event committee prepare for the upcoming Winter Ball, but after all that had been going on at the school, the Headmistress had advised it was best he took some time to be with his family. Zeke was skeptical that he would have much of a break if he went home.

"Now is the opportunity to make amends with your family," the Headmistress had said. *"Share all that you've learned from Once Upon Academy. They cannot deny that you are not the same young man they remembered."*

Zeke had given in with that newfound perspective and left for home. Despite his apparent curse—that had still not manifested—he felt in tip-top shape. His shifter abilities made for fast healing, and part of him wondered if they might've eradicated the curse entirely.

As he trudged up the steep hill, he looked out toward the vast Yukon tundra of the Canadian northwest, an endless land where his wolfpack clan, the Greyvalk, had taken residence for several generations. Scores of snow-tipped evergreens blanketed the white landscape, reflecting the northern lights that danced in the dark sky in a prismatic array of abstract designs.

It was still as beautiful as Zeke had remembered two years ago, before he'd left for OUA. He remembered many nights of the full moon, when he and his family would engage in the Running, a family ritual that honed their shifter abilities and let their inner beasts run free. The Running was older than the Greyvalk bloodline, which stretched all the way back to Germany and medieval Europe. It was the only time in Zeke's life where he'd felt unified with his family.

But those days were long gone. Zeke's fate was sealed the day he'd failed his strength test against his youngest brother, Louka. Zeke had lost his place in succession within the clan, as his failure indicated he wouldn't be capable of handling the responsibilities as one of the clan's protectors. He gritted his teeth. *I bet*

I can take him now, he thought. But second chances from the Greyvalk clan were few and far between, thanks to his notorious father.

Zeke shut away his anger for a moment and awed the scenery of his former home once more. He inhaled the crisp, evening air, saturated with the smell of fresh wood and evergreen. The skies continued their majestic dance of varying gradients of blues and purples. Finally, Zeke continued his trek to the summit where the Greyvalk cabin resided, overseeing the rest of the world below.

The trees around him rustled, and his ears perked. He looked around cautiously, not stopping his walk. He saw nothing. Although he was in his human form, his nose was able to pick up the vague scents of wolf. He was getting closer to home. Suppressing his nerves, he lifted his head high and focused his gaze straight ahead, steeling his nerves. *I'm not afraid,* he mentally chanted. Whoever was watching him would have a hard time sensing his fear.

The rustling continued, but Zeke continued his trek. His gaze darted back and forth, following the sounds. His wolf senses were on alert. Fear was an afterthought. Now, he was determined to confront his unseen visitor.

"I know you're there," Zeke said aloud to his unknown watcher, not stopping his walk. "Come out and face me, if you dare." He waited a few moments, looking around and listening, but no one accepted his offer. Zeke smirked. "Just as I thought."

At last, he reached the entrance of the grandiose, wooden, three-story cabin without incident. Approaching the stairs leading up to the threshold, Zeke glanced at the cabin's exterior. Not much had changed. There was a small, snow-covered recess on the ground in the front, where Zeke and his siblings used to wrestle as kids. The big oak tree that sat next to it bore faint claw marks in the trunk, from the many times Zeke would climb to the top during his reconnaissance duty.

The mixed memories encouraged a small smile that tugged the corner of his lips as he stopped at the front door and set down his duffel bag. His smile was short-lived, however, when the door suddenly opened and he was staring up at his eldest brother, Courtney. Zeke widened his eyes. Courtney was built like a brick wall, his mass nearly taking up the entire doorway. His T-shirt clung to his muscles so tight, they stretched at the seams. Zeke had no doubt that Courtney would be the clan's next successor.

Courtney looked him up and down and sneered. "What are you doing here?" he said, crossing his thick, defined arms across his broad chest.

Zeke swallowed back the tightness in his throat, then took a deep breath. "I'm back to make amends—and prove my worth."

Courtney snorted. "I doubt Dad will give you a second chance. I know I wouldn't. Once a weak pup... Always a weak pup." He stepped away from the door.

Zeke waited a moment, wondering if Courtney was really letting him in, or if he was going to attack him, or just slam the door in his face as soon as Zeke took a step. But when he noticed Courtney head into the kitchen, Zeke exhaled. He picked up his duffel bag, and slowly entered. He was immediately engulfed in the cabin's inviting warmth, courtesy of the big fireplace in the common room burning brightly. The cabin's interior was inundated with all the familiar smells of *home*. The mouthwatering aroma of cooked meat filled his nostrils. He'd come just in time for dinner. *Mmm. Sure hope Mother is making bacon-stuffed meatloaf tonight.*

As Zeke was about to close the door behind him, two grey wolves bolted inside and surrounded him, the hairs on their backs raised like spikes. Noting the white, star-shaped patch atop one of the wolves' heads, and the small, petite stature of the other wolf, Zeke recognized them as Elania and Dulce, his two sisters. The two wolves circled Zeke like prey, giving him a hungry once-over.

Dulce, his youngest sister, snarled, her golden eyes reflecting a magical shimmer. *"At least you didn't get any uglier,"* she projected in Zeke's mind.

Zeke scowled. "But you apparently got more annoying," he retorted aloud.

Elania, his older sister, wrinkled her nose, baring her fangs. *"You shouldn't have returned, Zeke."*

He regarded Elaina coolly as her emotionless voice echoed in his mind. "That's my business," he answered aloud. "I'll deal with it my own way." *I'm done being afraid.* He paused, gritting his teeth as he struggled for his words. "This… is my home…" he forced out.

Elania's ears perked up. *"You've changed."*

He spun and marched out of the common room. "You all better not have destroyed my room," he muttered. He suddenly bumped into someone stepping in his path. His body tensing, Zeke looked up. His middle brother, Warren, stood before him wearing a mischievous smirk on his angular face.

"You had a room?" Warren chortled, eying Zeke up and down. Warren was the sly and crafty one of the family. He had the looks, the brains, and also shared their mother's innate cooking skills. No one took him seriously, because *he* took nothing seriously. His carefree attitude, and his ability to talk his way out of any situation, had earned him his position as the pack's Omega.

Zeke frowned at Warren, then shoved past him. "Out of my way," he grumbled, crossing a small hallway and entering the kitchen.

Courtney was waiting in the massive kitchen, a luxurious, mahogany-themed getaway equipped with the latest appliances and technology for serving large gatherings. He stood at the preparation counter next to their mother, Mara. Her eyes downcast, the slender older woman carefully folded strips of bacon around a large hunk of beef in a pan.

Zeke quirked a smile at his mother. Unlike the rest of his family, Zeke held a place in his heart for her. She'd expressed her compassion discreetly, like making his favorite dishes or joining him during a family running, ensuring he didn't fall behind the others. Being mated with the Big Bad Wolf had its challenges, but Mara was cunning enough to hide her emotions in plain sight. Zeke knew and saw through her subtle charade. He just wished that she would have been more supportive of him during the darker times when he'd clashed with the rest of his family, and especially when he'd lost his fight with Louka. It seemed that day changed everything, including her.

Only two years had passed, but Mara appeared to be the same beautiful woman as Zeke remembered. Streaks of white accented her long, flowing jet-black hair, which contrasted perfectly with her creamy skin. She was thin and athletic, still as spry as a young pup.

Zeke's smile grew. He wasn't sure what made him happier: seeing his mother again, or the fact that she was making his favorite dish.

Courtney shot Zeke a cool gaze, then gently nudged Mara and whispered something in her ear.

Mara stopped her bacon-wrapping and looked up. Her jade-green eyes fixed on Zeke at the doorway, widened a moment, and then transitioned to a hard stare. "Ezekiel," she said, returning to her work.

Zeke started. Rarely had Mara ever called him by his full clan name unless something had upset her. Apparently, the two years apart from his mother had widened that rift in their relationship even more. Zeke had always gone out of his way to appease her. It was the least he could do as payback for all the times she'd shown her love. After losing his fight with Louka, Zeke worked twice as hard to win back his mother's honor and support. But now, it seemed, all of his efforts were futile. "Uh, hi, Mom. I'm back..." he muttered, scratching the back of his head.

She returned her attention to her work. "And what have these past two years taught you?"

Zeke stiffened. "Plenty... Aren't you happy to see me?"

"That is yet to be determined, cub," she said coolly.

Courtney smiled smugly at him.

Zeke pursed his lips. He wanted to believe that this was another one of her emotionless charades, but something deep inside him sensed a genuine inflection in her tone. *Have I lost you, too, Mother?* he thought, feeling the back of his throat tighten as own mixed emotions began to enter his mind. "Where's Pop?" he finally asked, hoping to steer the conversation away from himself.

"He is out on a reconnaissance mission," Mara replied, not looking up from her work.

Zeke blinked. "And you're not with him?" When it came to hunting and scouting, his parents were inseparable. If their outings ran past dinnertime, Warren was usually the one tasked with the cooking.

"Louka is with him. It's part of his training," she said simply. "Things have changed around here, in case you hadn't realized. However, if they are not back by the time this meatloaf is done, I'll be out there, too."

Zeke arched an eyebrow. "Since when did Pop start engaging in one-on-one time with his kids?"

She hissed. "It's not one-on-one time, Ezekiel."

"We're at war, little brother," Courtney added.

Zeke opened his mouth then closed it. *War?* The last time he remembered his clan being at war was when he was still a young pup. At that time, his family's territory was threatened by the presence of a mountain lion clan. Thankfully, his parents and elder siblings managed to defeat the intruders, and their territory hadn't been challenged since.

"What's going on around here?" Zeke finally asked, looking between his mother and brother.

Mara didn't respond, so Courtney continued. "A grizzly bear clan has taken up residence at the base of the mountain, openly challenging our father into conflict. One of them had the guts to steal food from our garden. We've been preparing, biding our time for the right moment to strike. We will show them why we sit at the top of this mountain.

Zeke grimaced. "Grizzly bears?"

"That's right, and you came at the right time to prove your worth—that is, if Pop will even bother to allow you a chance at redemption."

"We will need every able body to fight, so that will not be a problem," Mara said, laying the last piece of bacon across the uncooked loaf of beef.

Zeke clenched his jaw. *I didn't expect to be fighting in a clan war. Am I really ready for this?*

"Huh. Well, I'm not afraid," Courtney said. "None of us are. We're going to eradicate that clan."

The front door burst open, and an elk-sized grey wolf barged in. Zeke's father was as menacing as his name entailed. He was as big as he was strong, and the Alpha wolf's golden eyes glowed with menace. Spots of his frazzled fur were matted with blood, as though he'd been in a brutal fight. He took one look at Zeke, and his golden orbs narrowed to thin, glowing slits. Afterward, he growled, then padded down the hallway and up a set of stairs.

"Dinner will be ready in an hour, dear," Mara called, setting the meatloaf in the oven.

Tromping through the front door was a smaller wolf, who bore a white, diamond-shaped fur patch under his left eye. Zeke stiffened at the sight of his younger brother, Louka. The wolf was thin and scrawny, much smaller than Zeke. Louka looked at him, amused. *"Can't get enough of this place, huh?"* he jeered in Zeke's mind. *"Why did you bother coming back, anyway? Looking for another beating?"*

Zeke hissed and moved out of his brother's line of sight. He mentally swore for conceding to Louka's taunts. Zeke couldn't stand to look at him, especially now, seeing as Louka was literally the runt of the litter. *How could I have possibly let someone like him beat me in battle?* It was then he realized why his mother was upset with him, and why his father wanted nothing to do with him. If Zeke wasn't strong enough to defeat the weakest-looking member, he wouldn't be strong enough to protect his family, his name. *Maybe it's true. I'm too weak for this clan...*

Courtney smirked at Zeke's fluster, then left the kitchen. Walking past Zeke, he shoved him aside with a violent bump of his shoulder.

Zeke stumbled, but didn't retaliate. Not like he would stand a chance against him.

Courtney was quite the instigator, though not as bad as Warren. Still, Courtney always had to make it known which sibling was in charge. After he left, Zeke returned his attention to his mother. They were alone now, and somehow, Zeke was terrified of that. "So, uh… when is this battle supposed to go down?"

Mara looked at him dubiously. "Any day. Any minute. Any second. War is unpredictable, cub."

He chewed his bottom lip. The idea of war both frightened and excited him. Maybe coming back home wasn't a mistake. It was a way to make a renewed commitment to his family and gave him one last chance to prove himself, despite what happened in the past. "What does that mean?" he asked his mother. "Do we have to live on the edge of our seats constantly, waiting for something to happen?"

"No. You learn to balance life and survival. Has Once Upon Academy not taught you anything?"

"It's taught me plenty. We'd be here all night if I told you everything."

A small smile crept upon her lips. "Well, if and when we survive this, you can tell me all about it."

For a moment, Zeke sensed the kindly woman from two years ago. It warmed his heart to think that maybe she was still there, after all. "Of course," he said.

She began cleaning up the preparation counter. "We weren't expecting you to come back, to be honest. Your room's been converted into a gym."

He nodded. "I understand. I'll find a comfy spot in the basement or something."

She stopped wiping the counter and smiled. "Yeah, your favorite hiding spot. Fair enough. If you want to sleep down there, no one's going to complain."

He mirrored her smile, relieved that she'd recalled one of his few positive childhood experiences. The basement was his sanctuary whenever he needed to get away from his siblings, or the troubles of the world. He'd often hid among the storage boxes, where he could be alone with his thoughts. "Thanks," he said.

She gave him a small dismissive wave. "Your father will be back in a few minutes. I suggest you leave now while you can. He's not in a good mood."

When is he ever? Zeke thought, resisting the urge to roll his eyes. He understood his mother's subtle warning. He and his father never saw eye-to-eye before, nor did it appear they would now. In his father's eyes, Zeke was a failure, having lost his fight to Louka. Zeke had seen enough disappointment in one day, and he knew his father would be overly harsh in his criticisms. He decided to save himself the stress and leave the kitchen quickly. He opened a door in the hallway to a set of stairs that led down into pitch-blackness.

"Don't miss dinner, Ezekiel. Like always, it's first come, first served," Mara called from the kitchen.

Zeke sighed. Being home again had zapped his appetite, despite his mother making his favorite dish. He decided to forego dinner and be alone with his thoughts about tomorrow's plans. War was coming, and he had to be ready, come morning. He closed the door behind him and descended the stairs. His wolfish night-vision activated immediately, allowing him to navigate through the darkness. Reaching the bottom of the stairs, Zeke scanned the large area of storage boxes. Tucked in one corner was a door leading to the laundry area. Zeke remembered many times in his youth when he used to hide out in there. For now, however, he sought refuge behind a tower of cardboard boxes that looked like they hadn't been moved since all those years ago. He set his duffle bag down and sprawled out on the concrete floor, cold, hard, and smooth. He rested his head on the duffle bag as a pillow and stared up at the ceiling. *So this is home...*

CHAPTER 7

"THEY'RE HERE!"

Zeke's eyes shot open at the sound of Elania's shrill voice cutting through the floorboards above. He bolted upright from the basement floor. The aches in his body from sleeping on the hard concrete were suddenly gone as his heart began to race. *Did I have a bad dream?* he wondered, looking around the dark basement warily. Noticing the area was still dark outside the tiny egress window in the laundry room, Zeke realized he hadn't slept for long—perhaps maybe an hour.

The ceiling thumped with several sets of footsteps scrambling about. The tiny hairs on the back of his neck raised, as his protective wolf instincts suddenly kicked in.

Zeke blinked again. *The grizzly bear clan? Here? Now?* Tension flooded the air, making his throat tighten. Whoever these bears were, they must've been formidable opponents to cause his pack to go into such a panic. *This is my chance,* he thought. If he could hold off the intruders, he would surely be welcomed back into the pack. Even his father wouldn't be able to deny his son's newfound courage.

The pounding footsteps ceased, and all was quiet. Zeke realized he was alone. *Had they forgotten I was down here?* Part of the Greyvalk Pack's creed was that the whole pack fought for the clan's honor during times of war. *The whole pack...* He ground his teeth. *They don't believe in me. They never had and never will.*

One thing OUA and the Headmistress had taught him was self-confidence. It was time to stop living in the shadow of others and bearing the weight of their dismissive opinions. His family might have overlooked him, but he would make his presence known loud and clear and prove his worth. Whether his family liked it or not, he was still of Greyvalk blood. This was his home, this was his family, and he would defend them all with his life.

Zeke raced up the basement stairs two at a time and reached the kitchen. It was empty, and the table was full of half-eaten plates of meatloaf. *Shocking.* No one in his family ever left a drop of food—especially meat—on their plates. The matter was indeed serious. Zeke rushed out the front door.

Distant wolf howls pierced the air. Zeke started. *The Greyvalk battle cry.* Under the dim glow of the almost-full moon, Zeke discerned several figures, some big, some small, scrambling about. Low, guttural growls shook the ground.

Zeke ran toward the sounds. He concentrated on his shifting as much as he did the destination of the battleground. He tore off his shirt and tossed it in a bush he zipped past. The dizzying feeling of vertigo came over him—an odd feeling he had never before experienced whenever he shifted. He stumbled, his footsteps faltering. He shook off the sensation, regaining his bearings, and willed himself to push forward again. As his muscles enlarged, so did his frame, and he ripped out of his pants. Forced to all fours, he charged ahead, faster. Greyish fur covered his olive skin, and his senses became more acute. When his wolf transformation was complete, the dizzy sensation passed. He regained his bearings and his keen eyes locked once more on the battle scene ahead. The bears had besieged his family in strength and numbers.

Raising his head toward the sky, Zeke let out an echoing howl before bolting into the thick of battle. Feelings of fear and doubt dissolved in his mind in that moment, replaced by a focused anger that had been trapped inside him for so long. It was time to unleash that anger on his enemies.

The other Greyvalk wolves darted through and around the bears, remaining a moving target and keeping the grizzlies frustrated. The bears seemed unaware of his arrival.

Zeke fixated on the closest enemy, which also happened to be the largest bear of the group. Dulce ran circles around him, her small size making her agile moves lightning quick. But she was no match for the grizzly's cunningness, who was already two moves ahead of her. The next she moved within his range, the bear's massive paw had already swung out to meet her, smacking Dulce to the ground and pinning her with his weight. Dulce yelped and cried. The bear lifted his paw again, sharp claws aimed at her neck. He let out a low, guttural growl, as Dulce yelped again and attempted to squirm away. The bear's eyes locked on the helpless wolf, but he didn't proceed with the kill, seemingly waiting for her submission.

Noticing the bear's hesitation, Zeke took that small window of opportunity. *Now's my chance to save Dulce.* Jaws open and claws extended, Zeke latched onto the grizzly's hind leg. The unsuspecting bear howled and backed off of Zeke's fallen sister. The bear's muscles tightened and tensed in his grasp. Zeke locked his jaws and sunk his teeth deeper, until he felt the warmth of blood.

The bear whipped around, trying desperately to knock Zeke away, but Zeke continued to hold tight. Movement in Zeke's periphery zipped in his direction, then disappeared. Moments later, his father appeared and pounced on the bear's back. His father's eyes were dilated and filled with anger, and he became lost in his violent fury. The bear lost interest in Zeke, focused on defending himself from his new attacker, who relentlessly tore at his back with claws and bites. At last, the bear managed to shake the alpha wolf off his back. The wolf crashed against the trunk of a tree, and moments later, he was back on his feet.

Zeke caught his father's gaze, and the alpha wolf narrowed his eyes. *"Either fight or get out of the way."* Zeke heard his father's commanding voice in his mind.

Zeke backed away from the scuffle, as his father had that situation under control. Another bear had broken past Louka, Warren, and Courtney, and bounded Zeke's way, roaring, saliva oozing from his jaws. Zeke studied his opponent's movements carefully, waiting until the bear was only a few feet away. He noted the multiple, severe wounds that the bear had sustained, along with his strained movement and the limp in his back leg.

The bear pounced, massive sharp claws outstretched. Zeke bolted out of his opponent's strike zone and zipped behind him. Zeke leapt onto the bear's back, and drove his claws into the bear's sides, burying them deep into his ribs. The bear howled and collapsed, blood seeping out from multiple wounds. Zeke finally let go and stood in front of the bear, looking down at him. The bear raised his head weakly, his dark brown eyes regarding him with trepidation.

Zeke growled, baring his fangs, and crushed his paw onto the bear's throat. The bear whimpered.

"We... concede...." the bear projected in Zeke's mind.

Zeke started, and did a double take. It was the first time he'd ever heard such things from his enemies, as most battles tended to end in a certain bloody death. He slowly released his paw from the bear's throat. *"Leave our territory and never return. Next time, you will not be spared,"* Zeke mentally warned the bear.

The bear gave a weak nod. He hobbled to his feet and let out a weak roar, calling the rest of his clan. The other bears cowered back, some barely standing. They began to slowly draw back from the wolves, and eventually the battlefield.

Zeke and his family watched them carefully. Zeke noticed his father's body tensed and crouched low, as though he were about to chase after them. Zeke stepped in front of his father's path. His heart pounded as he stared face-to-face with the Alpha, and a shiver of fear ran down his spine. *"Let them go, Pop. They've conceded,"* he projected to his father's mind.

His father snarled. *"And you believe them? You have a lot to learn."*

"They've seen and felt what we've done to them, including their Alpha. I doubt they will be foolish enough to challenge us again," Zeke assured.

The Alpha wolf's eyes narrowed, and Zeke could sense pure evil swarming in those orbs. It seemed his father had other intentions. *"Those bears have no honor. No respect. I will show them why I rule this mountain,"* he projected. He bounded past Zeke, chasing after the bears.

Zeke turned away. He couldn't bring himself to watch—or hear—what his father intended to do to them. He was the Big Bad Wolf—bloodthirsty and merciless. Zeke looked at his mother and the rest of his siblings. Courtney and Dulce were bloodied with fresh open wounds, and they hobbled weakly with their tails between their legs. Warren lay on the ground, panting heavily, his fur matted with blood.

"Why didn't you kill him, son?" Mara asked.

Zeke lowered his head. He thought of all the reasons why, but it was a jumble in his head. He didn't want to be like his father. He didn't want to be a part of this war. He wished he hadn't come home. Finally, Zeke lifted his head, and stared into his mother's questioning eyes. *"Because sometimes, people deserve another chance."*

She sneered. *"You've forgotten what it means to be a Greyvalk in times of war. Never spare the enemy."* She turned and began heading back to the cabin.

Warren watched Mara a moment, then looked back at Zeke. *"Well, at least we still won, so…"* He struggled to his feet, lifted his head and howled at the moon. Then he hobbled after Mara. The rest of Zeke's siblings followed suit, giving their victory howls, and then returning to the cabin.

Zeke remained alone with his thoughts for a few moments. The sounds of battle, and the nearby deathly cries of the bears echoed in his mind. He didn't need to see what was happening to know what his father was doing to them. Unable to take the sounds any longer, Zeke broke into a sprint back home. *Did I do the right thing?* he thought as he ran. Deep inside, it felt right, but he apparently couldn't be any more wrong. His family was already inside the cabin by the time Zeke returned.

Warren, who was back in his human form and wearing nothing but a towel around his waist, appeared in the doorway. His wounds were already closed and scabbed over, thanks to his fast healing. "You coming in or what?" he called, wearing a big grin.

Zeke regarded Warren with slight surprise. It seemed Warren wasn't upset about the way Zeke handled things at the battle's end. Maybe it was the fact that Zeke was brave enough to stand up to their father, something none of his other siblings had ever dared to do. *Have I finally earned Warren's respect?* Zeke wondered.

"Here." Warren tossed him an extra towel.

Zeke concentrated on his shifting. The vertigo feeling returned, this time stronger than ever as he began assuming his human form. His muscles cramped, and as he rose on two legs again he staggered around like a toddler, unable to keep his balance. He grunted at the effort. "Oh man, my head's spinning..." He picked up the towel and awkwardly secured it around his waist.

Warren's eyes grew saucer-wide. His jaw dropped open. "What the—?"

Zeke leaned against a support post on the cabin's front porch, held his head, and groaned. His senses were all off, including his balance. *That battle must've really taken a lot out of me*, he thought.

"Guys! Come quick!" Warren called inside the cabin. "Zeke is…"

Moments later, the rest of the family joined Warren at the front door. They looked toward Zeke and their faces turned pale, their shocked expressions matching Warren's.

Zeke scrunched his brow. "What are you all looking at? What's wrong?" He looked down, hoping the towel hadn't slipped off—it was still there, thankfully. However, something else caught his attention: his feet. They were covered in grey fur. He blinked and felt his face, which was furry as well. He looked at his hands. They were human hands, but, like his feet, they were covered in grey fur. His nails were also longer than usual. *Oh no… What's happened to me?* The horrified look on his family's faces echoed his sentiment.

Mara shook her head solemnly. "I never thought such things were possible…"

"What's happened to him?" Louka asked, cocking his head.

Zeke approached one of the cabin's front windows and peered at his reflection. His face and body was an amalgamation of human and wolf, as though he'd somehow managed to stop in the middle of his shifting. He gulped. *I... I'm a monster!* "Wh-what's going on?" he asked his family.

"You're a defect," Mara said, her gaze hardening. "A shifter who can't fully shift is useless."

Zeke huffed. *A defective?* He'd only heard about such things from scary children's bedtime stories his parents and older brothers used to tell him when he was a young pup. *Can such a thing be true?* "N-no. This can't be. I've always been able to fully shift before. Why is this happening now?"

"I knew there was something different about you when you came back," Mara said. "You're cursed, Ezekiel."

Curse... Zeke gasped. *Is this Tilda's doing?*

"How did he become cursed?" Dulce asked, looking from Mara to Zeke.

"Who knows? It might've been dormant in him all his life," Mara explained. "It was only a matter of time before it would make its presence known. Everything that has happened with you over the years now makes sense. Your father was right to have distanced himself from you when you were young. It seemed he already knew the truth. And now, so do we."

Zeke widened his eyes. His heart pounded. "W-What are you saying, Mother?"

She pointed down the mountain. "Leave now. Leave before your father returns. He will kill you."

His mouth went dry. Zeke's dreaded nightmare had returned, and now had become a reality. "But, Mother, I can fix this…"

She shook her head solemnly. "This can never be fixed. It is who you are."

"No…"

Mara's eyes dulled and then became glassy. She turned her back to him before he could spot any more emotion from her, and disappeared inside. His siblings' gazes turned more cautious.

Courtney folded his arms and puffed out his chest. He regarded Zeke with a stern gaze. "You heard her. Go. Defectives have no place in our clan. Leave, and don't come back, or I swear I will kill you before our father does."

Zeke's eyes burned, as the image of his incredulous family wavered. *So this is it. Just like that, I'm alone again.* He turned to leave, then looked over his shoulder. His siblings remained crowded at the doorway, watching. With a sigh, Zeke turned away from his family and began heading down the mountain, not looking back.

CHAPTER 8

ZEKE RAN THROUGH THE THICK, snow-covered evergreen forest wearing nothing but a towel around his furry, half-man-half-wolf body. He was sure he looked ridiculous, and, despite everything, part of him was grateful that that nearest town was several miles away. Zeke's bare, furry feet plodded through the snow until his body finally collapsed from exhaustion. He crawled to a nearby tree and leaned his back against the sturdy trunk. He looked down at his furry hands, which shook. *What sort of magic is this?* he wondered.

Why can't I fully shift anymore? A shifter that couldn't shift was a failure. A defective.

He'd finally had the courage to return home after two years in hopes of making amends with his family and proving himself, but all he did was make things even worse than before. He was truly alone from everything—and everyone—he knew. He dreaded returning to OUA. He'd either be the most feared student there, or the biggest laughingstock of his peers.

A bitter cold whisked over Zeke's face, and he shivered. The Canadian winters were brutal—yet another thing he didn't miss about home. He drew his knees to his chest. He was so far from the nearest town, he'd probably die of exposure if he attempted the treacherous trip. Then again, his chances of survival were slimming the longer he stayed huddled in the middle of the forest. His mind and body were exhausted; he didn't know what to do. *Maybe it's best I go back to OUA. At least they have hot chocolate,* he thought, trying to stop his chattering teeth. Returning to the school was only an incantation away. Fairy Godmother had taught him the Recall spell during his orientation.

He began uttering the words between chatters, but as the cold continued consuming him, he found it hard to concentrate on the words. He slowed his speech to individual syllables. The final words to the spell were on the tip of his tongue, when another chilly gust blew, picking up flakes of snow. The gust carried a strange burning cold that froze him instantly. Zeke's body had gone completely numb. His weary form slumped over, and his eyelids drooped. Slowly, his exhausted mind slipped further away from consciousness. The world around him faded away into darkness. He took a slow, deep breath. *So this is how I die...*

Amid the pitch-blackness in his mind, Zeke noticed a small beam of white light shine down in front of him from somewhere above. The light cast a warm, illuminated ring on the ground, easing the chill in his bones. A ghostly image of a woman appeared in the light. The specter slowly solidified and stood before him, her black-painted lips turning crookedly to a sinister smirk.

Tilda! Zeke seethed at the strikingly beautiful dark-haired woman, who melded into the surrounding voids with her long black dress. His burning anger warmed him from the inside and reinvigorated him. Zeke tried to move his body, but an unknown force held him in place. He let out a growl in protest.

Tilda glided to him in a single step—a graceful, innocent gait that masked her evil. "I love your new choice of fashion, Pup," she jeered, nodding to the towel around Zeke's waist.

"You!" He snarled, attempting to move his body again. She was within arm's reach, and yet, he was unable to touch her.

She chuckled mockingly and casually tucked a stray wisp of black hair behind her ear. "Did you really think I would let you get out of this that easily?"

He gritted his teeth. "Where am I? What are you doing here?"

"You're dead, silly," Tilda replied with a casual flick of her wrist. "Well, you would've been, had I not arrived. The timing of the curse's manifestation couldn't have been more perfect."

Zeke blinked. *So it* was *the curse!* "H-How did—"

"—I know where you were?" Tilda finished, smiling sweetly. "Ever since you had been afflicted by that curse, you've been like a shining beacon. I've always known where you were. I've watched you sulk and drag yourself around Once Upon Academy before finally working up the courage to return home. Pity, your family turned their backs on you. We have much in common, Pup."

He stared at her, wide-eyed. "You knew? You saw?"

Tilda quirked a smile. "Indeed. However, it was only until the curse manifested that I was able to physically come to your location." She knelt before him and tilted his chin up, forcing him to look at her. "That look is very becoming of you, Zeke. Reminds me of a certain beast-man I used to know." She chortled.

Zeke whipped his head back and forth, looking anywhere but at her. "Don't touch me, witch! Get this curse out of me, now!"

"I rather like you this way. And I'm sorry, dear Pup, but I cannot lift the curse."

Zeke blinked. "What? But it's your spell."

"It is, though once the spell has been cast and the curse has been applied to its target, it is literally—and figuratively—out of my hands. But the good news for you is that there is a way to break the curse. The bad news is you will probably not live lone enough to find out."

He huffed. "I'll spend the rest of my days finding a way, and once it's been lifted, I'll be coming for you."

She tsked. "That's not very gentlemanly of you, dear Pup."

"I'm not a gentleman to evil witches like you," he said, narrowing his eyes.

"*Touché.*" Tilda smirked. "Well, if you are in that much of a hurry to get rid of the curse, then perhaps it is not something you should go about figuring out alone. Why not implore some of your peers from Once Upon Academy?" She perked up. "Ah! You should pay a visit to Perle. I am most certain she would be willing to help you with your little matter."

He bristled at the sound of Perle's beautiful name uttered from that evil woman's mouth. "Leave Perle out of this."

"You know, it was her book that caused your curse," Tilda said in a casual tone.

"*You* gave her that book!" he retorted.

"She didn't have to accept it."

He growled. *It's a trap. It has to be.* He fought the invisible restraints again. He was trapped in this dark world with Tilda, helplessly at her mercy. "I am not leading you to Perle," he said.

"I don't care about Perle," Tilda said, rolling her eyes. "My interest lies in one man—my first love. Soon, I will see him again, and we will be married."

Zeke curled his lip. Tilda seemed incapable of love. He pitied the man who had garnered that woman's attraction.

Tilda stepped away from Zeke and returned to the ring of light. "And now, I shall be off. I advise you to find yourself a nice warm place for the night. I might have spared you from a certain icy death once, but next time, I may not be in such a good mood." Smiling, she winked, and her image became ethereal once more, then disappeared.

Alone again, Zeke felt the warmth of the light subside, and the bitter chill of the tundra lands quickly return. The icy sensation trailed throughout his body again, seizing his veins. Gasping, Zeke opened his eyes and bolted upright against the trunk of the evergreen tree. *I'm back,* he thought, scanning the snowy lands around him. He felt in control of his body again, and his energy returned. *Did she bring me to that nightmarish place? Can she see me now?* He pursed his lips and scanned the area for Tilda, looking, listening, and sniffing for her presence. When she didn't appear, he sighed with slight relief. *Maybe she can't do that spell that often,* he desperately hoped. Still, knowing that Tilda was keeping tabs on him kept him unnerved.

His understanding of arcane magic was limited, and his conversation with Tilda disturbed him. It was time to consult the Headmistress with this new information. Hopefully she had figured out how to lift his curse. Rather than get Perle involved, like Tilda had hoped, he would implore the grand mistress of magic, herself. And while Zeke remained hidden, the rest of the school would continue with the Winter Ball—an event he had never dared to attend, even before the curse.

Zeke closed his eyes and concentrated on the Recall spell. He envisioned the bustling, mahogany halls of Once Upon Academy. He envisioned the Headmistress's office: her desk, the two plush chairs, the shiny red apple on her desk. They were small details that helped to enhance the spell's effectiveness. The sights, smells, and sounds all came to him vividly, as if he were there. Seizing those images, he uttered the spell's incantation.

A few minutes later, a gust of snow flurries appeared in the distance at the forest entrance. The white veil lifted and a glowing white pumpkin carriage appeared. Zeke squinted and noticed the carriage, which was pulled by a majestic white Arabian horse, heading in his direction. *Right on time,* he thought, hugging his body tight to fight off the cold. He stood, readjusting the towel around his waist.

The carriage arrived, and the driver, who was dressed in an ornate, purple-and-gold-trimmed Victorian-style box coat disembarked. The driver appeared unaffected by the weather, as the light snowflakes that fell over him, the horse, and the carriage quickly melted before they could penetrate. He took one look at Zeke and furrowed his brow. "Ah… you called for a carriage, Mr. Wolfson?"

Zeke studied the man, noting his slightly shocked expression. He could only imagine how his friends and the entire student body would react. *I'm not going to break this curse by staying afraid,* he thought. He took a deep breath, mustering new courage. "Yeah," he replied to the driver. "I need to go back to OUA. Now."

"We have arrived, Mr. Wolfson," the carriage driver announced.

Zeke fluttered his eyes open. The trip back to Once Upon Academy felt instantaneous as soon as he had entered the carriage. He'd fallen asleep on the comfortable plush seat as soon as his head had hit the headrest. It had been a long, grueling night, and he was glad to be out of that nightmare and back at a place he had deemed his sanctuary. He stared at the school's exterior with trepidation. It was mid-morning, and class exams were still in session for a few more days. He was grateful to have finished his exams early, but he didn't expect to return to the school so soon. Then again, he wasn't expecting a happy outcome with his family, either.

Zeke was grateful that the carriage came equipped with a spare OUA uniform: a pair of black slacks, a matching woolen vest branded with the school's Pegasus emblem, and a white button-down shirt. A pair of black shoes sat beneath the clothing, along with a matching pair of dark-grey socks. It was a relief to be out of that dreaded towel, but the uniform wouldn't be enough to hide his hideous features.

The driver opened the carriage door for him. He inclined his head, though his gaze discretely traveled to Zeke. He cleared his throat, and then pursed his lips.

Growling, Zeke narrowed his eyes at the flustered man. "What are you looking at?" he demanded.

The driver started, then straightened to attention. "Ah, n-nothing, Mr. Wolfson. We have... uh... arrived at Once Upon Academy, sir."

"Yeah, you said that already," Zeke said, stepping out of the carriage. He stood in front of the shallow staircase leading up to the grand double doors of the school's main entrance.

The driver rushed back into the carriage and sped out of the cobblestone driveway.

Alone, Zeke felt his heart beat faster. *No turning back now.* No escaping the fallout of this curse—or his current fate. He clenched and unclenched his fists, then slowly trudged up the stairs, keeping his head lowered.

He pushed open the front door, and the scent of old mahogany rushed out, filling his nose. Many students traversed the halls, rushed to and from exam rooms, chatted in small groups, or hung around attempting some last-minute cramming. Two students sat in the study area with their heads down, deeply engrossed in their notebooks. No one seemed to notice him; perhaps this was his chance to slip in and reach the Headmistress's office unnoticed.

He walked with long, fast strides, keeping his head down and his furry hand covering the side of his face. His ears perked at the low murmurs around him.

"Hey, who's that?" someone nearby asked.

"New student?" another said.

"What is he, some kind of wolf?"

"I'm sure Zeke would love that..."

Zeke felt his throat tighten. He broke into an all-out sprint, foregoing his shoddy job at concealing his face. He whipped around the corner and shuffled up the stairs. His eyes stung as he traversed the halls leading to the Headmistress's office. A mix of fear and panic burned his insides. He finally reached the Headmistress's office, only to discover that the door was locked. He huffed, defeated.

"No... no no no no...." he muttered, tugging on the locked door. There was no keyhole or physical lock on the door, which indicated that the doors were magically sealed. There was no way he was going to get inside. Zeke let out a deep sigh and rested his forehead on the door.

"Mr. Wolfson?"

Zeke lifted his head and looked over his shoulder toward the source of the soft voice. Fairy Godmother stood before him, an aura of sparkling white light surrounding her stout frame. She wore a powder-blue suit jacket over a white blouse, and a knee-length blue skirt. A thin, white wand was held delicately with her fingers. She tilted her head slightly, her creamy face regarding Zeke with grave concern.

Zeke kept his back to her, too embarrassed to reveal his grotesque features. "Ms. Fay. I need to see the Headmistress. It's important."

Ms. Fay stepped closer to him, her steps soft and silent, like a cat's. "The Headmistress is not here at the moment. But perhaps I can help you."

"No, I don't think you can," he said quickly. He felt her gentle hand touch his shoulder, and he winced.

"Don't underestimate my power, Mr. Wolfson," Ms. Fay said. "I know about your curse. I have been working closely with the Headmistress to find a solution."

He chewed his bottom lip and shifted his gaze sideways. "And?"

"And…" She pulled him around, forcing him to look at her. She narrowed her eyes, staring deep into his as she studied him closely. "It is not a curse that can be lifted by conventional means."

Zeke shuddered. Apparently the woman wasn't fazed by his appearance. Relief and joy spread through his bones. Ms. Fay saw beyond his frightening exterior. She was truly pure and good in all things. "So what are you saying? I'm going to remain like this forever?" he asked.

She shook her head. "Once upon a time, Tilda cast a similar spell on a former student here. She was in love with him to the point it drove her mad. Ironically, it was his heart that broke the curse."

Zeke scowled. "Are you saying that evil witch is in love with me?" He shuddered at the thought.

"I don't think so. However, there could be some connection with this curse... and where your heart lies."

He made a face. "My heart doesn't lie anywhere but with myself. Not even my own family. I don't trust anyone."

"Are you?" Ms. Fay lifted a thin, grey eyebrow. "Out of all the students here, only one has asked me to check on you during the break. Perle Durand has a very big heart, especially for you. Even if you don't realize it."

He blinked several times. *Perle was really worried about me?* His heart swelled. Why she would still be concerned with someone who hadn't reciprocated those same feelings baffled him. And yet, his heart thrummed delightfully at the thought. His lips parted, as he felt inclined to reply, but he was rendered speechless.

Ms. Fay's expression softened. "Even just mentioning her name has changed your demeanor considerably. I think it is safe to say where your heart truly lies. And that is how you will break this curse."

Zeke thought about Tilda's words. *Maybe she was right...* She'd been coercing Zeke to see Perle, but he was certain it was a trap. *But why would Tilda want to help me destroy her own curse?* He thought again. Perhaps it would mean Tilda getting closer to Perle's father. Zeke couldn't let that happen. "I want to see Perle, but..." Zeke told Ms. Fay his thoughts.

She nodded slowly. "That makes perfect sense, and why you need to avoid Perle's father, Beau, at all costs."

Zeke shrugged. "How can I do that? Perle will most likely be with her father."

"Your task is to talk to only Perle and try to get this curse lifted. Find a way to get her alone and away from her father, if you must."

"All right. I understand. I will see Perle and break this curse, and I will make sure I avoid her father."

She clapped her hands together and smiled. "Wonderful. I can send you there." Her smile faltered. "It is such a shame that all of this has to happen so close to the Winter Ball in three days."

Zeke grimaced. "I am definitely *not* going to the ball. I wouldn't be caught dead like this: a half-shifted monster. I don't need any more ridicule than I've already gotten from my own family."

Her gaze hardened. "It is against the ethical code of the school to ridicule or harass another student. If that ever happens to you, please do let me or the Headmistress know immediately."

If only if it were that easy. Earning respect amongst his peers was one of the hardest things Zeke had ever done since he became an RA. He was a leader. What kind of leader couldn't control their own powers? It would only be a matter of time before his peers would see past his charade and realize that maybe he had never been a leader at all. *Maybe my family was right. I'm a defective...* He sighed deeply, shoving the dark thoughts aside. "I'm ready to go."

"All right, relax," Ms. Fay instructed. She waved her hand in the air, creating a swirl of sparkling light that trailed from her fingertips. "Close your eyes. When you open them again, you will be in France."

CHAPTER 9

PERLE HAD NEVER SEEN SO many ball gowns in her life. But at her father's behest, he'd ensured she had nothing but the best. No dress shop in the world could compare to the variety and exquisite, professional quality of Candlewick's Boutique. Her daytrip to Paris with her father ended up being more productive than she thought. Beau knew the owner of Candlewick's Boutique so well that the owner offered a same-day turnaround service exclusively for him, through the use of magical means, of course. The owner offered this special service exclusively to Beau as a way of showing gratitude, after Beau had single-handedly saved his youngest son's life from a house fire. Of course, it also helped that Beau was his top customer and gave the biggest tips.

By the end of the day, Perle had walked out of the shop with five tailor-made dresses she had absolutely fallen in love with. She looked forward to wearing each of them at all of Once Upon Academy's formal functions.

"You know, I would've been happy with just one dress," Perle said to her father as they drove back home.

He snorted, not taking his eyes off the road. "Absolutely not. You are your mother's daughter. You two change your minds faster than the wind blows. Now you have no excuse. You have a dress for every mood."

She chuckled, then decided to end the conversation on that note, knowing that arguing with her stubborn father was only a losing battle. She peered in the backseat at Nuit, who was curled up, napping. He hadn't budged from that spot while Perle and her father were shopping.

It was mid-evening when they arrived back in Riquewihr. Perle stared at the passing landscape of the endless vineyards, rolling hills, and wildflowers that glowed under the bright moonlight.

"Whoa!" Beau exclaimed.

The sound of screeching tires jolted Perle from her thoughts. Beau slammed on the brakes, and she jerked forward suddenly. Nuit yowled and hissed. Still shaken, Perle looked at her father, who stared straight ahead."

"What's going on?" she asked, then followed his gaze. There was something large in the road—something large, like a man's body...

"*Mon dieu...*" Beau put the car in Park and jumped out.

Perle watched him approach the mysterious person. *A furry person.* She hopped out of the car and joined her father. Nuit followed.

Beau knelt and shook the stranger. "Hey! Hey! *Ça va?*"

The stranger's body lolled lifelessly.

Perle watched Beau roll the stranger onto his back. She noted his clothes, which bore the emblem of OUA on the breast of the shirt. And there was something awfully familiar about his face—it was a wolf mixed with a human's, but she could sense something distinctive about him. Her eyes widened, and she gasped. "Z...Zeke?"

Beau snapped his gaze up at her. "You know him?"

She nodded. "*Oui.* He goes to OUA with me. He's one of the RA's. He risked his life to help me stop Tilda before. But what's happened to him now? He looks... different."

Beau studied him. "He looks like he could be a shifter, but he somehow got stuck in the transition. That is not normal. Let's take him into town. I have a friend there who knows healing magic for shifters." He reached down to scoop him up, and then Zeke's eyes suddenly shot open. Beau jerked back, dropping Zeke.

Zeke recovered and crawled to his feet. He was slightly shorter than her father, but similarly built. Greyish-white fur covered his body, a jumble of human and wolf traits. He stared at Perle and Beau, his eyes emanating an eerie purple glow. His gaze lingered on Beau, and he growled.

Beau threw his arm in front of Perle. "Get back to the car. Now."

Perle hesitated. She whipped her gaze between Zeke and her father. "But—"

"Now!" Beau's voice boomed.

She felt a panicked sensation from Nuit project into her mind. Her familiar raced back to the car, and she scrambled away as well. She glanced over her shoulder back at the stand-off between Zeke and her father. Zeke had an awkward gait about him, as though he were not in control of his own movements. His eyes continued to glow a deep purple, unlike the beautiful golden hue she'd remembered of him. *What's happened to him?*

Zeke suddenly burst out laughing. The familiar cadence of the cackle gave Perle goosebumps, and she halted her retreat as she reached the car's door handle.

Tilda!

"At last, I have you exactly where I want," Zeke said in a voice that didn't quite sound like his own.

Beau growled. "What is this?"

Zeke collapsed to the ground. Purplish smoke began sublimating from his still form, before coalescing into a vague human form. Suddenly, an image manifested above Zeke's body. A tall, lithe, feminine figure dressed in black. The ghostly image became whole and solid, and she stood before Beau. She looked down her nose at him, her dark eyes pinning him with haughty desire. A smirk was etched across the icy features of her face. "Hello, again, my love."

She's back! Perle's mind raced. *How did she get here? What has she done to Zeke?* Perle wasn't sure how the dark fairy got here, or what she had done to Zeke, but she knew she had to do something fast before she hurt not only Zeke, but her father, as well.

"Hey!" Perle shouted to Tilda. "Leave him alone!"

"Stay back, Perle! *Fais ce que je dis!*" her father barked.

"Yes, that's right, little Perle. Do as your papa says." Tilda jeered with a chuckle.

Perle felt her cheeks burn. She turned away from the car door. *I can't let that evil woman hurt the people I care about again.*

Tilda extended her hand to Beau. "Come, my love. Let us get away from here and catch up on old times."

Beau snarled and stepped away from her. "If you think I'm going anywhere with you… you… witch!"

Perle rushed back to stand with her father, with Nuit dashing with her a few paces behind.

Smirking, Tilda swept closer to him as fast as the wind. Beau started, and Tilda wrapped her arms around his waist. Her arms emanated a dim, purple glow.

"Let go of me!" Beau demanded. Growling, he tugged and squirmed in her grasp, trying to break free. The purple light brightened around Tilda's arms, as though the magic was feeding on his resistance.

Tilda hugged him tighter. "I always loved your take-charge attitude. Come with me on a journey." The purple light appeared around her body like a halo. The glow crawled from Tilda's form to encompass Beau, as well.

"Papa!" Perle called, reaching out for his shirt as the purple light intensified. The image of the couple began to fade. Perle's fingers grazed the knit fabric of Beau's shirt sleeve, and she was suddenly engulfed by the same purple glow. She could no longer feel her father's shirt, and the entire material world around her began to change. The purple light was blinding, but she knew she was no longer in France.

The light dissipated, and Perle found herself alone in a dark, hazy void. The air was cold and crisp.

"Papa?" she called, her voice echoing throughout the smoky abyss.

Nuit meowed in response, and the cat emerged from the haze, trotting to her.

She gasped and scooped him up. "Oh, Nuit... Where are we?"

He jumped out of her arms and looked around warily.

The cloudy haze they had arrived in began dissipating, and Perle found herself before a wall of massive thorny vines covered in bright-red roses. A pleasant, sweet smell filled her nostrils, contrasting with the lingering feeling of despair and doubt surrounding her. The scent brought memories of home, and her father's coveted rose garden. But she knew she was far from home. *Is this a dream? Another spell? ... A curse, perhaps?*

She noticed an opening in the wall, which led to a maze of more of the dreaded thorny vines that twisted and turned every which way. The wall of vines stretched high in the sky. There was no telling how vast this maze really was. She called for her father again, but it went unanswered. *I have to find him.*

Nuit squeezed through the wall's opening, and Perle followed. They began traversing the strange maze. The smell of the roses was heavenly, and, rather than a distraction, was a constant reminder that her father was still in trouble. Soon, the top of a tall structure came into view in the distance, still obscured by the wall of vines. It was the first different thing she'd seen since arriving in this strange place.

Nuit suddenly sprinted ahead. Perle rushed after the cat. "Wait! Not so fast!" Perle huffed.

Nuit continued running, turning at specific corners and deftly jumping over or dodging the menacing thorns that blocked the path. It seemed Nuit knew exactly where he was going. The cat was far ahead now, but still in her sight. *"You know where Papa is, don't you?"* she projected to her familiar. She received a warm and reassuring sensation from the cat. Smiling, she picked up the pace. She carefully crawled under low-hanging vines and hopped over small ones blocking the path.

At last, she reached the center of the maze, where the towering castle turret stood. A curtain of rose vines covered the turret's entrance and wrapped around the structure's weathered brickwork, spiraling upward and stopping beneath the window at the top. Beyond the window's amber-hued flickering candlelight, Perle spotted two silhouettes.

Nuit squeezed underneath the vines and made it to the entrance of the turret. Instead of a door, another wall of thick, thorny vines blocked the opening. Perle approached the wall and frowned. *Papa may be in there somewhere. I have to find him.*

Perle concentrated on her Fire Hands spell. The words and somatic motions came to her immediately—her hands warmed and were suddenly engulfed in magical flames at her command. She placed her flaming hands onto the wall of vines. The sizzling flames snaked through the plants, feeding on them eagerly until the vines blackened and withered. Afterwards, she pushed through the weakened vines, and entered the turret. The entrance was dimly lit with a shallow set of stone stairs laying before her, spiraling upward.

Perle kept her fiery hands burning bright as she climbed the stairs two at a time, using the flames' light to help her navigate through the darkness. Nuit kept up with her, scampering a few steps behind. Midway up the tower, Perle felt her legs burn. She glanced down the endless spiral into the dark pit below. Her heart pounding, she hugged the wall closer. *"Stay close to me,"* she projected to her familiar. *"It's a long way down."*

Nuit meowed and rubbed his cheek reassuringly against her calf.

A wave of renewed courage and determination filled Perle's mind.

Adrenaline rushed through her bones. She continued her ascent. *I'm coming, Papa…*

At last, Perle reached the top of the stairs. She leaned over and panted, catching her breath. She stood before a closed wooden door.

"We are to be married, you and I," Tilda's muffled voice crooned.

Beau growled. *"Non! Jamais!* I will never marry you. You will never have my heart."

"You will love me. I will see to that… by any means necessary."

Papa! Perle gritted her teeth. She placed her hands onto the wooden door and summoned her fiery spell. The door gushed into flames. The fire hungrily dissolved the wood, uncovering Beau and Tilda standing inside a majestic, red-rose-themed throne room with tall windows that were shrouded with sheer, white curtains. Two high-backed golden chairs with red padded seats were set on a raised platform in the middle of the room. Rose flowers and petals were scattered everywhere on the floor and furniture.

Large tapestries depicting rose images decorated the stone walls.

Beau sat in one of the chairs, his arms and legs bound by thorny rose vines that protruded from the stone ground. Blood trickled from his arms and legs, where the thorns punctured his skin.

Nuit hissed, arching his back. The cat's distress amplified Perle's own. "Papa!" Perle called.

Beau gasped and looked over his shoulder. "Perle! What are you doing here?"

Tilda narrowed her eyes at Perle. "How *did* you get here?"

"You brought me here," Perle said, scowling at the dark fairy. "Leave my father alone."

Tilda chuckled. "You and your foolish wolf pup helped me enough, reuniting me with my love. I have no more use for you. As far as I'm concerned, Beau never had a daughter."

Beau grunted. "Get out of here now, *fille!* You cannot handle her" he called to Perle.

Perle gritted her teeth, ignoring her father's warning. Seeing him in distress only fanned the fire in her hands, causing them to grow brighter, hotter. "Let my father go. Now," she warned.

Smirking, Tilda extended her hand toward Perle. A green ball of swirling light coalesced in her palm.

Something sharp suddenly scratched Perle's leg. Thorny vines began growing out of the cracks in the stone floor near her feet, shooting toward her and sprouting smaller tendrils that spiraled around her ankles. She gasped and leapt out of the way of the aggressive vines that pursued her. Perle grasped one of the reaching tendrils with her flaming hands and singed it to ash. The vine retracted, as if in pain. Seeing her chance, she grabbed a larger part of the recoiling vine with both hands and enveloped the plant in flames.

Tilda left Beau's side and hovered in the air before Perle. Dark purple magic swirled around the dark fairy. "Looks like you've gotten stronger since we last met." A large glowing prismatic ball of magic grew from a pinpoint over her hands, and she began chanting an incantation in a voice that was both hers and something more sinister.

Beau struggled and growled, but the vines continued to hold him tight. The vines constricted in response to his resistance, the thorns digging deeper into his skin, and he cried out.

The sounds of her father's cries tore Perle from her focus on stopping Tilda to rescuing her father. In the end, Perle conceded to the pain and despair on her father's face. She rushed to his aid, carefully placing her hands over the binds and burning them away with the flames swimming from her hands.

Tilda's eyes burned white as she remained in her trance-like state chanting, focused on unleashing her powerful spell. She held the large prismatic ball of energy high above her head.

As soon as the last bind was burned away, Beau recovered his footing and rushed at Tilda with unnatural speed, his bestial rage taking over. Snarling, he lunged at Tilda, tackling her in the air. Tilda's prismatic ball of energy fizzled out as her spell was interrupted. Beau and Tilda clashed, and the momentum of Beau's charge sent them both tumbling out one of the large open windows.

Perle gasped. *Papa!* She extinguished the magical flames from her hands and rushed to the window. Her father was grasped onto the window ledge with one hand, his fingertips white as he fought with all of his strength to hold on. Tilda wrapped her arms around his legs for dear life. Far below them was the endless sea of vicious thorny rose vines.

"I'm not... letting you go...." Tilda said in a weakened voice. "If I can't have you... no one will..."

Beau reached up with his other arm, and Perle pulled with all her might. "Ungh... Why do you have to be... so heavy, Papa..." she muttered through strained breaths.

Beau grunted and grasped more of the ledge, until he was able to pull his torso up, with Perle's assistance. He kicked his legs, attempting to shake Tilda free, but she remained stuck to him like glue. "Let go of me, witch!" he growled.

Tilda grunted. "You're mine, Beau... Together... even in death..."

Perle heard the distress in the woman's voice. Tilda was weakened considerably. Becoming interrupted in the middle of a casting a spell sometimes had detrimental effects on the caster, depending on how strong the spell was. Tilda was at her most vulnerable, and that was the time for Perle to strike.

Tilda's delusional heart was blacker than night. She was beyond redemption, seeing as she was willing to take the people she 'loved' with her to the grave. With that thought steeling her nerves, Perle invoked the power of electricity in her hands. Small streaks of lightning danced between her fingers. "His heart will never belong to you, Tilda," she said to the woman. She held up her fist, which crackled with an electric shimmer. "You've hurt so many people. Now you're going to be trapped in your own illusionary world forever."

Tilda sneered. "You can't... take me... from him..."

"Watch me." A tickling sensation traveled up Perle's arm from the buildup of static electricity. For a moment, she thought back to her final exam, and the little white target on the dummy's forehead. Ms. Fitcher's lecture echoed in her mind. *"Small target. Center. You see everything."* Perle stared at a small spot in Tilda's center mass—*seeing* Tilda, taking her in—and soon Tilda's face crystalized in her periphery. Locked on her true target, she hurled the summoned lightning bolt toward Tilda's face. The force of the electric blast jolted Beau all the way through the window, while Tilda's grip was yanked away. Tilda fell toward the thorny pit below, her screams echoing throughout the land. The thorns impaled her mercilessly, and her screams were silenced.

CHAPTER 10

ZEKE OPENED HIS EYES AND looked up at the two blurry faces looming over him. *Am I still dreaming?* He thought. The last thing he remembered was leaving OUA after talking with Fairy Godmother. His mind was in shambles after that.

Then he heard a cat's meow. He focused on the two blurry faces, and his vision soon became clearer. He recognized one of them. A woman. *Perle.* His heart pounded. *Why is she here? Wait... wasn't I just talking to Ms. Fay? Ugh. What's going on?*

"Zeke?" Perle whispered in a soft voice. Her black cat, Nuit, approached him and licked his forehead.

Zeke shuddered at the cat's sandpaper tongue, and growled, gently swatting the animal away. He looked at the other person, an older man with a somewhat rough edge to him. He was tall with a hefty build, and there was something slightly familiar about his dark eyes.

Zeke swiveled his gaze back to Perle. He slowly sat up and grunted. "P...Perle..."

Perle beamed, her adorable bright smile making his heart swell. "*Oui*. It's me. Are you okay?"

The older man narrowed his eyes at Zeke, then looked at her warily. "Be careful, *fille*. Her dark magic may still be in effect."

She nodded. "Yes, Papa."

Zeke blinked. *Papa.* Well that explained why the man looked familiar. He rubbed the back of his head, trying to remember bits and pieces of his conversation with Fairy Godmother. "Am I... in France?" he asked.

Perle's brow furrowed. "*Oui*. What are you doing here?"

"I came... to see you..." Zeke muttered.

Her eyes widened slightly. She fell silent.

Zeke swore under his breath. *Did I say something wrong? Or maybe she's completely disgusted with me right now...*

Her father relaxed his body a little, and he extended his hand. "Can you stand? Do you need a healer?" he asked Zeke.

Zeke looked at the offered hand, and then shook his head. "No, I'm fine. I'll heal better on my own." He grunted and slowly stood.

The man retracted his hand. "I know all about that, *mon frère*. But even shifters have their limits when it comes to injuries."

Zeke regarded him with a raised eyebrow. "You're a shifter?"

"I was, once upon a time. And in some ways, I still am."

"That doesn't make sense." Zeke shook his head.

The man chuckled. "Says the shifter who can't shift."

Zeke bristled.

Perle touched Zeke's shoulder. "Don't bother arguing with him. You'll never win. Come on. We'll bring you back to the house."

Zeke's irritable nerves were instantly calmed by Perle's soft touch. The tension in his shoulders eased, and he exhaled a deep sigh. He turned his head away. "I shouldn't have come here," he muttered.

Perle cocked her head. "Why? I'm glad you're here. I'm not sure what's happened to you, but…"

"Don't look at me…" he said quickly.

"Maybe I can help you, if you'll let me," she said reassuringly.

"Enough," her father's voice boomed. "We'll return to the house at once." He folded his arms across his broad chest and pinned Zeke with his hard gaze. "And since you are a friend of my daughter, then I don't expect any problems from you, no?"

Zeke gawked at the man, noting the edge in his tone, and the pointed gaze that seemed to establish his dominance in this group. Zeke nodded slowly. "Yes, sir."

The man cracked a coy smile, and his demeanor returned to calm again. "Excellent. Well, let's be off, then."

The three of them piled back in the car and continued on to the house. Zeke sat next to a neatly stacked pile of clear garment bags containing fancy dresses, which he guessed were Perle's. They were beautiful, and reminded him of the dreaded Winter Ball fast approaching. They rode for several minutes in awkward silence. Zeke took the time to think about his purpose here. Soon, he remembered. *The curse.* And Perle was most likely the key to breaking it. Zeke wasn't sure what to say, or how to explain his situation to her. Perle had helped him too many times before in the past, as well; asking her for yet another favor made him feel selfish.

And now that he was in the presence of her intimidating father, Zeke knew he had to be extra careful with his words and actions.

The car stopped in front of a quaint cottage, which sat amid a vast vineyard and garden. Zeke was the last to get out of the car. He gazed at all the different types of vibrant plants, amplifying the beauty of this stunning place. There was no way to grow half of these things in the frigid Yukon. Zeke inhaled the mixed scents that surrounded this place, which all had an underlying scent of roses. All of it made him think of Perle.

The front door opened a crack, and Nuit meowed and scampered inside. A woman came to the door wearing a yellow housedress and white apron. "Beau? Perle?" she called.

Zeke studied the woman carefully. She had an infectious smile on her smooth, flawless face. The kind of addicting smile that was reminiscent of Perle's. More than her smile, the other distinguishing features of her almond-toned face were unmistakable. *That must be Perle's mother,* Zeke figured. It was no wonder Perle looked so perfect in his eyes. She bore every one of those stunning traits from her mother.

"*Oui,* Jolie." Beau replied, carefully unloading the garment bags from the car. "And we've company." He motioned to Zeke.

Jolie furrowed her brow at Zeke. "Ah… *Bonjour.*"

Zeke inclined his head, though her insistent staring unnerved him.

"Mother, we have news," Perle said in a grave tone.

Jolie pursed her lips. "Let's talk about it inside. I made some tea."

The four of them gathered around the kitchen table, enjoying a cup of chamomile tea, while Nuit was nestled happily in the corner enjoying some canned tuna. Zeke stared in horror at Perle and Beau as the two of them recounted the terrible events of the day: how they were whisked away by Tilda's dark magic to some strange land, and Perle was forced to battle—and defeat—the dark fairy on her own and save Beau. Zeke wasn't sure why he couldn't remember any of that. *Did Tilda cast some sort of spell on me? Or maybe it's part of this curse...* Zeke should have been there to help them defeat Tilda. Or at least to protect Perle and her father. But it sounded like Perle was more than capable of handling herself.

"So... it really was Tilda all this time," Jolie said, when the story was finished. She lowered her teacup to the saucer.

Beau snarled. "I can't believe she had continued to wreak havoc on my life. After all this time, she was still bent on a non-existent affair."

Jolie pursed her lips. "That was one disturbed woman. She was obsessed to the point of insanity."

"Who would've thought a simple 'hello' to her one day would've brought upon all this mess?" Beau shook his head. "From now on, I'm keeping my big mouth shut."

Jolie smirked. "I'll drink to that."

Zeke looked around the table. "Does that mean Tilda is gone for good? *Really* gone for good? OUA is no longer threatened by her evil?"

"I think so," Perle said. Then, her expression dulled. "I saw her die... She fell from the tower... impaled by those treacherous vines. There's no way she could've survived. And I'm pretty sure it wasn't another one of her illusions."

"We must inform the OUA staff about this immediately," Jolie said. "Tilda is gone. That is great news."

Zeke stared blankly at his full cup of tea. He hadn't taken a single sip from it. "Tilda is gone, and yet, I'm still... like this." He felt his face. "I'm still cursed. I'm still a monster."

Perle exchanged glances with her parents, and then looked back at Zeke. "You're not a monster, Zeke. You're the bravest, most handsome and kindest man I know."

Zeke looked at her dubiously. "Don't try to console me, Perle. I know I'm hideous. I can't go back to OUA looking like this. Everyone will know that I'm a shifter that can't shift. I'm a defective."

Perle reached over and took his hand in hers. She rubbed it reassuringly. Her warm, gentle touch sent a revitalizing surge through his entire body. She looked at him with deep compassion in her dark eyes. "I don't care how you look, Zeke. You're still a great man."

"No," Zeke growled, snatching his hand away.

"Do you disagree with what my daughter thinks about you?" Beau pinned him with a hard gaze and taunting half-smile.

Zeke swallowed. "No, sir."

"Papa..." Perle shook her head at him. Beau rolled his eyes and went back to enjoying the rest of his tea. Perle returned her attention to Zeke. "It's okay, you know."

Zeke idly traced invisible lines on the table with his finger. "I remembered why I'm here." He paused and looked back at Perle. "I came because you may be the one to help me break this curse.

Perle's face lit up with slight shock, then softened. "Of course, I'll help you."

His heart thrummed. "It may take a long time to figure out the cure."

"It doesn't matter. I'll help you, regardless." she smiled.

Zeke nodded slowly. Perle agreed now, but would she really stay committed to that promise for possibly years to come?

"Maybe there's something at OUA's library," Perle continued. "I'll return to the school early and start researching." Her expression dulled. "Since... you are not going to be attending the ball, then I guess I'll have some time on my hands to research."

Zeke grimaced. "Yeah, I wouldn't be caught dead at the ball looking like this."

"I understand. I just wish things could've been different. I was hoping that maybe... we could've gone together. "

Zeke shook his head firmly. "Absolutely not." He paused and bit his tongue, suddenly realizing what he'd said.

The table and teacups suddenly shook. Beau rose from his chair, his tall, foreboding frame looming over Zeke. "What exactly are you saying, Zeke? You don't want to take my daughter to the ball?" He glared.

Zeke chewed his bottom lip, Beau's sharp tone making him straighten to attention. He wiped his sweaty palms on his lap. "Oh, no, sir. I just... uh... don't feel worthy to take your daughter to such an exquisite ball."

Jolie smiled softly. "You know, Beau was like you once—proud and self-conscious. But he also had a big heart—for me. Tilda put a spell on him, turning him into a monster, and yet, I still fell in love with him because he had a loving and caring heart. We've been inseparable since, and I never looked back." She finished her tea and stood. "My advice, Zeke? Worry less about your outward vanity, and more about your heart. Think about the others around you. That is what truly makes you beautiful, inside and out." She took Beau's hand and led him out of the kitchen. "Come on, Beau. Let's leave them to talk alone and catch up on things."

Beau glowered at Zeke one last time, then reluctantly followed Jolie out of the kitchen.

Once they were gone, Zeke heaved a deep sigh of relief. He didn't want to admit that perhaps Jolie was right, but he couldn't shake off the memories of his heartbreaking encounter with his so-called family that rejected him for his appearance and inability to properly shift.

"Your parents are special," Zeke finally said to Perle. "I can see where you get your kindness and strength. My vanity is perhaps my weakness. I don't like being different. Not when it's such a drastic change like this. And I'm not just talking about the way I look. People fear things that are different because they don't understand them.

"I can't face the entire student body like this. They won't understand what's happened to me. To them, I'd just be a shifter who can't shift. How will I ever be taken seriously again? I'll lose my respect in a heartbeat."

"You won't lose your respect," Perle assured. "Being different isn't a curse. Besides, it'd be awfully boring if everyone looked the same all the time."

"You know what I mean," Zeke said flatly. "I don't want to be a half-shifted monster. I want to be me again. I want to be in control of my powers again."

Perle looked thoughtful for a moment. "I'm not sure how I can help you reverse this curse, but I'll do whatever I can."

"You should enjoy yourself at the ball."

"My friends are more important than a ball."

His gaze averted to the table and his untouched tea. She wasn't going to the ball if he wasn't. *Why is she punishing herself like that?* Her words, so full of genuine care and compassion, stung the mixed emotions in his mind. He was still afraid to fully open up his heart to her—to be the vulnerable wolf his family thought. She was the last spark of goodness that warmed his heart. And yet, he didn't want to lose her like he'd lost his family. *Why was this so hard?* "I... I can't stay here anymore. I'm going to go back to the school."

She frowned, and then nodded slowly. "All right. I guess I can't stop you. I will come see you soon, okay?"

"Yeah..." He stood up from his chair.

"I wish you would stop running away," Perle muttered as he was about to leave the kitchen.

He stopped and looked over his shoulder. "These days, it's all I know how to do." He trudged out the front door, with the Recall spell on the tip of his tongue.

To his relief, Perle didn't stop him.

CHAPTER 11

ZEKE STOOD BEFORE ONCE UPON Academy's grand entrance once more. The last of the final exams had concluded, and the campus was gearing up for the Winter Ball tomorrow evening. Snow-themed lights, garland, and other décor graced the building's exterior, as well as the light poles that surrounded the main driveway and illuminated the campus. In just a few days, this place had already transformed into something right out of a winter-themed storybook—a story that Zeke had no intentions of being a part of.

He trudged up the staircase and entered the main halls, now devoid of students, where the winter décor continued along the mahogany walls, floors, and ceiling. *So much for helping the event committee with the decorations.* He continued his trek toward the Headmistress's office, relieved that he didn't have to conceal his face from his peers this time. He silently prayed to the stars that the Headmistress would be there.

He reached the door to her office and exhaled a deep sigh. As his fingers graced the handle of the door, a dim light surrounded him and grew brighter. Retracting his hand, he stepped back and stared at the door. A shower of glittering white light appeared in thin air, forming the outline of a stout, feminine figure. The shimmering form solidified, revealing Fairy Godmother, holding her wand. She smiled at him warmly.

"Welcome back, Mr. Wolfson," she greeted.

Zeke inclined his head. "Hi, Ms. Fay. I… need to speak to the Headmistress."

Her smile broadened. "I know. She's here, and she's been expecting you. She is well aware of what has happened."

He blinked. "She is?"

The woman nodded and then waved her wand at the door. With a sparkling shower of magic that emitting from the wand, the doors opened. "Come," she beckoned.

He stared toward the Headmistress, who sat at her desk, and his heart pounded furiously. *She knows… Does that mean she has a cure for this curse?* he wondered. He followed Fairy Godmother, his heart swelling in anticipation. They stopped before the desk—the Headmistress was deeply engrossed in an old thick tome, among many others that were stacked on the desk, and even on the floor beside her. Meanwhile, Azure, her bluebird familiar, sang a cheerful tune from his wooden perch above.

Fairy Godmother gently cleared her throat. "Headmistress, Mr. Wolfson has returned," she announced.

The Headmistress looked up from her book, her smooth, creamy face brightening with their entrance. "Welcome. I'm glad you're back." She gestured to the high-backed chairs in front of her desk. "Please sit."

Zeke looked at the chairs with trepidation, then back at the Headmistress. This was the first time she'd seen him since the curse manifested. And yet, she appeared unfazed by it. Or maybe she just knew how to hide her feelings well.

Fairy Godmother beamed. "Well, then. I will leave you two to discuss matters. I will be in the grand ballroom, assisting the event committee with the decorations." With a swift wave of her wand, she disappeared in a poof of sparkling light.

Alone with the Headmistress, Zeke slowly approached one of the chairs.

"You've had quite an adventure these past few days, haven't you?" the Headmistress began, smiling cheerily.

Zeke tilted his head, unable to read her. *What is she really thinking?* "It's been terrible," he muttered, finally sliding into the seat.

"I know." Her cheery expression became softer and more compassionate. "But the main thing is that Tilda has been stopped for good. Her death echoed throughout the very threads of magic.

"If she's dead, then why am I still cursed?" Zeke asked.

"It is the last remnant of her dark power. Curses remain in effect even if the caster dies. That is why I, and many of my assistants have been tirelessly researching. And I believe I may have found the solution."

Zeke scooted to the edge of his seat. "You can break it?" His eyes widened with hope.

The Headmistress held up her finger. "Allow me to explain. I have been researching your condition extensively, ever since the day you were struck by the book's magic. That day in the summoning chambers... when I cast my disenchantment spell on the book, it had some sort of reverse effect. An enchantment was released from the book and sought a new host—which was unfortunately you. It was then I realized that this was no ordinary enchantment spell."

Zeke clenched his jaw. *So, in other words, I was in the wrong place at the wrong time,* he thought. *Now I understand what Tilda meant when she said my curse was a 'wonderful accident.'*

"When I learned of the curse's manifestation," the Headmistress continued, "I realized it was a form of entrapment spell that only applies to a polymorphed subject."

"What does that mean?" Zeke asked, furrowing his brow.

"It means the spell only triggers when the subject tries to change shape. It traps the subject in that changed shape. Indefinitely."

He rubbed his chin. "So that's why I'm trapped in my half-shifted form…"

The Headmistress nodded. "Yes, that's right. Incidentally, it is very similar to the curse that Tilda had inflicted on Beau Durand long ago. He's Perle's father, and was once a student here."

Zeke thought about his brief conversation with Beau. *So, that's what he meant about being a shifter.* "How did he break the curse?" he asked the Headmistress.

She looked thoughtful. "He had to love and be loved."

"What does that mean?"

"Beau was quite the ladies' man, though I could tell his heart was truly set on Jolie, Perle's mother. Jolie wasn't interested at first, seeing as Beau was always surrounded by female admirers, Tilda among them. Tilda was jealous and selfish, and knew how to use her magic effectively. She was determined to have Beau to herself. But when he rejected her, Tilda put a curse on him, turning him into a monster. She knew Beau loved Jolie, but Jolie didn't love him back. So, Tilda figured the curse would make Beau finally get over Jolie, and love Tilda instead for the affection she still showed him even in his cursed form."

"And since Tilda loved Beau, then, if he loved her back, the spell would be broken, right?" Zeke concluded.

The Headmistress nodded. "That's right. But of course, things didn't go as planned for Tilda. I believe we are faced with a similar situation now."

He blinked. "Wait… you mean…"

"Yes… you must love and be loved, unconditionally."

He sank back in his chair. There was only one person he cared about. But deep enough to the point of love? He wasn't so sure. Perle was kind and compassionate to him, but he doubted her feelings went any deeper than that. They were friends—classmates, and nothing more. He'd been pushing her away for so long because he didn't want her burdened with his problems. And yet, even with all his efforts, she still stood beside him. "That's impossible," he muttered.

"Love is never impossible, Mr. Wolfson. I know there is someone special who has made your heart flutter." The Headmistress arched a knowing eyebrow.

He rolled his tongue in his cheek. There was no sense in dancing around the subject. The Headmistress already seemed to know. "I like Perle. She's a friend. But beyond that? I don't know. You're asking me to desire someone beyond friendship."

"I'm asking you to listen to your heart," the Headmistress corrected.

He did listen to his heart—that inner desire to be with Perle, help her, and protect her—every time Perle became the subject of a conversation. His feelings for her did extend beyond friendship, but they were also shrouded in fear—fear of rejection and of vulnerability, the very thing he had spent his life trying to prove he wasn't. After what happened with his family, Zeke couldn't bear dealing with another loss. Besides, after meeting her parents, he wasn't sure if he would be able to live up to their daughter's expectations of what love should be anyway. "Even if I did love her, I don't think she would feel the same way," he muttered.

The Headmistress gave a dismissive wave of her hand. "Nonsense. I propose you talk to Perle about this together." Her expression brightened. "Ah, and what better time than during the ball! Now, that is where true magic happens."

He scrunched his nose. "I'm not going to the ball."

Her eyes dulled, and she pursed her lips. "I see. Well, I do wish you would reconsider."

"I've made up my mind. I'll just wait until after the ball to talk to Perle."

She sighed and looked back down at her book. "Well, I guess that's settled, then. I do wish you well, Mr. Wolfson. Just remember one thing: you are never alone."

Zeke stared at her with a sad gaze. The change in her tone of voice indicated that he was dismissed. He slowly rose from his chair. "Thanks for the talk, Headmistress."

She said nothing and continued reading.

Zeke swallowed, briefly thinking about their conversation. Then he turned and quietly left her office.

CHAPTER 12

PERLE DECIDED TO RETURN TO the school early the next morning, the day of the Winter Ball. Perle left home feeling bittersweet, as she wrestled with the decision of whether or not to attend the ball. Her parents understood and admired her willingness to help Zeke. Part of her, though, was still considering attending the ball. After all that her parents—especially her father—had gone through to get her the perfect dress, she didn't want to disappoint them by not wearing it at all.

Besides, it was such a beautiful dress, and she was anxious to wear it.

But Perle had no idea that these unfortunate events would befall Zeke. Deep down, she cared for the reserved wolf shifter, even when he tried to push her away. She assumed that he was angry at the world. She wondered about his family. Did they know about his curse? What if the people he loved turned their backs on him? She couldn't imagine how grim that life could be. But even in all the darkness of Zeke's situation, Perle was glad of one thing: Tilda was gone for good, and she would no longer wreak havoc on the lives of others. Perle's heart still pounded as she recalled those harrowing moments of her father's distress, Tilda's deathly screams, and the strange, yet powerful magical sensations that Perle felt burn deep in her core as she battled against the dark fairy. It was yet another aspect of Perle's magical abilities that she had to explore.

And even though Tilda was gone, Zeke's curse remained, which baffled Perle. She had decided to consult the Headmistress. After dropping off her gowns at her dorm, Perle made her way across campus to the main building. Nuit trailed a few paces behind her, swatting at random butterflies and insects that fluttered in his path.

As Perle reached the main door, she suddenly felt a strange tingling feeling in the back of her mind, jolting her to attention. She looked at her familiar, but realized the sensation was not coming from him. Nuit returned her look with curiosity. A bird's whistle cut through the air, drawing her attention to a small ledge over the entrance, where a bright blue bird was perched. Perle smiled, recognizing Azure, the Headmistress's familiar. "*Bonjour*, Azure," she greeted.

The bird whistled a happy tune, and the Headmistress's soft voice spoke into Perle's mind. "Welcome back, Ms. Durand. I am waiting for you in my office."

The empathic link was severed, and Azure flew away. Perle rushed inside, and stopped in her tracks when she saw the heavily decorated interior. She looked around in awe at the hanging white lights that twinkled like stars, and the wall tapestries depicting winter-themed scenes, and images of snowflakes. The floor was covered in pure-white magical snow that glittered in the light, painting a majestic picture of a fanciful world. Despite the hallway's comfortable temperature, the magical snow did not melt. It wasn't until she noticed the stairwell at the end of the hallway leading up to the Headmistress's office that Perle realize that she was still at Once Upon Academy.

Perle climbed the snow-covered stairs and approached the Headmistress's closed office door. She gave a few small knocks and waited. Moments later, the doors slowly opened on their own. The Headmistress sat at her desk, her glowing hand extended toward the door. She smiled at Perle. "Please come in, Ms. Durand," she urged.

Perle nodded and slowly entered. The Headmistress lowered her hand, and the doors closed. Azure flew inside the office from an open window and settled on his perch above the Headmistress's desk.

"Hello, Headmistress," Perle said, approaching the desk.

The Headmistress gestured to the high-backed chairs in front of her desk. "I am absolutely ecstatic to see you again. Word of your great deeds have spread throughout the magical realms."

Perle took a seat, and Nuit hopped in her lap. She regarded the Headmistress curiously, and then she realized. "Ah, you mean Tilda, yes?"

She nodded. "We are all eternally grateful for your courage."

"Did my father tell you?"

"No. Tilda's world resides within the threads of magic. Higher-ranking magical adepts like myself and Fairy Godmother have a strong connection to these threads, and therefore, we can sense reverberations within them. After we felt this disturbance, we were able to scry the source—Tilda—and saw the aftermath."

Perle rubbed her chin. "So, that world was real? It wasn't an illusion?"

The Headmistress gave a solemn nod. "It was very real. That was Tilda's realm. You have done so much in the short time you have been here, Ms. Durand. I cannot be more proud." She reached behind her desk and pulled out a small velvet box, then set it on the desk. "I want to commend you yet again on a job well done, and for the amazing bravery and ability you've demonstrated to defeat Tilda and save your father. And ultimately, save everyone at this school once again. You are only just a freshman, and yet, you have demonstrated powers that are more commonly displayed among the upperclassmen, and even some graduates. You possess a unique gift I have only seen in a few students."

Perle eyed the box, then felt her cheeks warm at the Headmistress's flattering compliments. "T-Thank you, Headmistress. But I believe I was doing what anyone else would've done. My father was in danger. I had to do all I could to save him from Tilda."

"Your humbleness precedes you." The Headmistress slid the box across the desk. "I had these specially crafted by some of my dwarven friends."

Perle stared at the box, then looked back at the Headmistress, bewildered. "A gift? F-for me?"

"Indeed." the Headmistress made a small head gesture.

She moistened her lips and slowly opened the box with shaky hands. Inside was a pair of exquisite gold earrings with small, intricately etched rose charms crafted from the purest rubies she had ever seen dangling from the intertwining gold chains. She ran her fingers along the jewelry. *Mon dieu...*

"These are absolutely beautiful!"

"My friends are experts in their craft. The earrings are also magical. When you wear them, the charms will emit a faint rose scent to remind you of home. When you touch one of the charms while wearing them, say the word *revenir*, and you will be transported back to your dorm room, no matter where you are."

Perle gawked at the earrings. "Amazing. Like my very own Recall spell."

"Indeed. And I think these earrings would make a perfect accent for your ball gown, yes?"

Her excitement quickly waned. *The ball...* She swallowed and slowly closed the velvet box. "Yeah... they would look nice..."

The Headmistress arched an eyebrow. "Something wrong?"

"I don't think I'm going to go. I... I need to help Zeke solve this curse. I'm going to do some research in the library."

Her smile broadened. "I believe we came up with a solution to Mr. Wolfson's curse. I think you ought to talk to him."

Perle regarded the woman dubiously. "Zeke isn't one for talks."

"You might be surprised at his current inclinations. And I do think you should reconsider going to the ball. It is your very first one, after all. You will be making memories."

Memories... Perle didn't want the memories of her first ball consisting of being unhappy knowing that Zeke was somewhere alone and miserable. "I don't know, Headmistress. I feel so selfish thinking of myself like that. Zeke is important to this school. He needs help."

The Headmistress sat back in her chair. "Ms. Durand, you are truly pure of heart. I trust you will make the right decision." She made a small dismissive wave. "You are dismissed now. I do hope I will see you later tonight."

Perle slowly stood, taking the velvet box with her. She considered putting them on and trying out the spell, but decided against it for now. The earrings reminded her of the ball, and she had too many conflicting feelings on that subject at the moment. Nuit, sensing her distress, projected assurance in her mind through his empathic link. She walked the rest of the way back to the dormitories while she tried to sort out her thoughts.

She reached her room and opened the door. Her mouth dropped open. The two people pressed against the wall of the kitchen with their lips locked suddenly looked her way. Eyes widening, they jumped a foot apart from each other, breaking the kiss.

"Anala? Ben?" Perle gasped at the couple.

Anala's face flushed redder than her wild hair. "Ah… h-hi, Perle. I… uh… just stopped by real quick to grab a few utensils I forgot. I'm, uh, on my way to the ballroom kitchen to get started with these desserts!"

Ben's cheeks matched his short hair, as well. "Uh, h-hello, Perle," he said sheepishly, rubbing the back of his head.

Perle looked at the both of them in disbelief. *Anala... and Ben?* She had no idea that they were a thing. *When did this happen?* "Um... I'm sorry for interrupting..." she stammered.

Ben cleared his throat, and slowly sidled his way toward the front door. "Uh, no. You're not interrupting. I need to pick up my suit from the tailor, anyway. See you tonight, heh." With that, he rushed out the front door in a blink.

Perle looked at her roommate and frowned. "I suppose I wasn't meant to know this secret?"

Anala blinked. "What? No, it's not like that. I mean, Ben and I... well, this thing just sort of happened in the span of a week. Ben asked me to the ball. I couldn't believe it. Ben Spriggan asked *me* to the ball! Of course, I said yes, but I warned him that I was a Dragon, but he didn't care. He's really been great, and he's not afraid. He even helps me out in the kitchen. He's a great helper, by the way. Oh! He's even thinking about taking up culinary class next year. Isn't that great?"

Perle stared at her blankly. She still couldn't believe that Ben of all people was interested in someone like Anala, especially when it seemed like he was afraid of his own shadow. He was certainly full of unexpected surprises. "That's wonderful, Anala. I'm happy for you," she said wistfully. She turned and headed for her room. "I hope you two have a good time at the ball."

"Oh, we will. I—hey!" Anala grabbed the back of Perle's arm, stopping her. "What's wrong?"

Perle deflated. "Nothing. I just have a lot of work to do..."

"Work?" Anala spun her around and looked at her with an arched eyebrow. "You're done with finals. You passed, remember? What's really going on with you?"

Perle chewed her bottom lip. "I'm not going to the ball, all right? Anyway, don't you have some cooking to do?"

Anala's eyes widened slightly, small flames flickering in her pupils. "Not going? Are you crazy? This is your first-ever OUA ball! You never stopped talking about it all semester." She paused. "Wait. You didn't get a dress, is that it? Well, no worries, we can go to the village and—"

"Oh, no, I've plenty of dresses. Please, don't worry about me. I'll be all right. You and Ben have a good time."

Her lips formed a thin line. "Is that what this is about? Me and Ben? I told you, it just sort of happened. And, uh... I also found out that he and I play the same roleplaying game. I had no idea we had so much in common. One thing led to another, and, well, here we are." Her eyes filled with worry. "I... didn't know you liked him, too..."

Perle blinked. "No, I don't like him. I mean, not like that. We're friends, of course. I'm happy for you two. But that's not what this is about."

Anala swept around Perle and stood in front of her bedroom door and crossed her arms, blocking Perle from continuing. "Then we should talk. I hate to see you like this. You're my muse, and I'm supposed to be concocting the perfect dessert for the ball. I can't look to you for inspiration when you're this depressed."

Perle slumped her shoulders, giving in to her roommate's insistence. She trudged to the dorm's common area and plopped down on the couch. Anala sat next to her and looked at her intently.

"All right, here it goes…" Perle rubbed her hands and kept her gaze averted as she told Anala everything, from Tilda's return to Zeke's dilemma.

When Perle finished, Anala sat back against the couch and gaped. "Stars! Now that's what I call an adventure! How come you get to have all the action? … I'm sorry to hear about Zeke. Can you really help him? I mean, he's not exactly the approachable type." She paused, looking thoughtful for a moment, and then laughed. "Haha, look at me, the pot calling the kettle black."

Perle smiled slightly. "I want to try to help him. He's alone. I don't think he has anyone to turn to. No family."

Anala nodded. "I understand. You're a good person, Perle. Zeke needs to get over whatever is bothering him and let people help him. Don't let all this stop you from enjoying yourself. The ball is only for one night, anyway. I'm sure Zeke will be okay stewing alone for a few hours. It's going to be so much fun, and I'm going to make the grandest, most exquisite cake you've ever seen!"

Perle's smile lifted a bit more. Anala knew just how to cheer her up. Maybe she was right. Perle could enjoy herself at this momentous event, and still help Zeke. And yet, a small part of her still felt guilty about that. She willed those negative thoughts aside and focused on her roommate with newfound excitement. "I thought you were making *Canelés de Bordeau?*"

"I did! They're in the ballroom kitchen's fridge, ready for tonight." Anala beamed.

"My culinary professor was so impressed with how they turned out, he offered to give me double extra credit for making a cake. Any ideas?"

Perle raised her eyebrows. "Double extra credit? I didn't think such things were possible."

"The perks of being one of his best students. All because of you being my muse, of course. So? What do you think?"

She tapped her chin in thought, and then perked up. "*Je sais!* Berry *Mille-Feuille* cake with Chantilly cream."

Anala's fiery eyes burned with delight. "Now, you're talking!"

CHAPTER 13

PERCHED ON A BRANCH OF a large oak tree in the courtyard, Zeke watched from a distance as scores of students made their way through the grand ballroom's entrance. Some students walked arm-in-arm, while a few entered solo. All of them were dressed in their finest gowns, suits, and tuxedos. The ballroom's exterior was transformed into a magical, lighted snow-themed palace, complete with a canopy of twinkling icicle lights strung overhead and paper snowflake decorations that hung from the building's tall windows. Colorful rainbow lights swirled in various patterns along the building's stone exterior. Elegant, fanciful music filtered out of the open doors, indicating that the ball was well underway.

Zeke sighed. He'd made up his mind to not attend, but he'd decided to dress up for the occasion, at least. If he should ever run into the Headmistress tonight, he could simply use the excuse that he was taking a break. But of course, he knew that's all it was—an excuse, and a bad one at that. For someone who was a son of the Big Bad Wolf, he was a terrible liar. He idly fiddled with one of the cuffs of his green overcoat. It shocked him that this suit still fit, since it was the first and only suit he'd ever owned since coming to OUA. His family didn't do formal events. He still couldn't believe he went through with this— dressing to the nines despite being a half-shifted monster. He gritted his teeth in annoyance, realizing he was a walking oxymoron.

He kept watching the entrance, hoping he might catch a glimpse of Perle all dressed up in her beautiful gown. Even though she'd told him she would forego the ball to help him, he didn't believe she would follow through. Tonight was too special for someone like her to miss. And Zeke would rather her enjoy herself instead of trying to fix something that was probably out of her control. *There's no way she would ever love me,* he thought.

His gaze caught sight of a group of women heading into the ballroom. One of them wore a yellow gown. He focused on her, and wondered if it was Perle. If he knew her, she would be wearing her favorite color to the ball. He straightened on the branch and stared intently, his heart thrumming in anticipation. He deflated when he realized that woman wasn't Perle, and frowned. *This is pathetic. What am I doing up here?*

Zeke spotted Ben and Anala walking arm-in-arm through the entrance. Anala leaned over and kissed his cheek. Zeke lifted an eyebrow. *Even that annoying clown found happiness tonight.* Zeke gritted his teeth. He knew all about Anala's relationship troubles. She was a nice girl who was just misunderstood. Maybe Ben was just who she needed.

"Meanwhile, I sit here sulking in a tree," Zeke grumbled to himself. He balled his fists and flared his nostrils. His siblings were probably laughing at him right now. His father, resting his case. His mother, turning her back on him. He let out a guttural growl.

I'm tired of running. I'll live with this curse if I have to, but I'm not going to run.

He dug his fingers into the branch, his sharp nails making small indentations in the bark. He took a final deep breath and climbed down the tree, smoothing out the wrinkles in his slacks and checking the gold buttons on his red vest after landing. He approached the fountain in the courtyard and stared at his wavering reflection under the light of a nearby lamp post. "I'm not the monster. You are," he said with a sneer at the ugly reflection.

The sounds of light footsteps tapping against the cobblestone made his wolfish ears perk. His throat tightened. Someone was coming. It was time to face his fears. It was time for his peers to know the truth. He slowly spun around. The universe suddenly stopped. His gaze lingered on a beautiful golden angel dressed in an exquisite gown that twinkled like tiny starlights.

It was Perle.

Despite her talk with Anala, it took every ounce of her willpower for Perle to convince herself to attend tonight's ball. Her heart ached as she made her way to the ballroom that night, with the fleeting hope that she might run into Zeke. But to her dismay, he was nowhere to be found. Thankfully, the rose earrings she wore had helped calm her nerves, since she'd dropped Nuit off at the ballroom's annex with the other familiars who were happily playing together.

Finally, as Perle was about to make her way inside the ballroom-proper by herself, she noticed someone lingering in the distance in the courtyard. A man dressed in a fancy suit. The faculty was inside the ball already, so Perle assumed this loner was another student. His back was turned, and he was staring intently into the fountain. *Maybe he is waiting for someone to show up, too.* Perhaps, if Zeke didn't show up, Perle could offer another one of her fellow students some company. At least she got to wear her gown tonight, after all.

She lifted her gown slightly and walked with careful steps down the path leading to the courtyard. As she neared the man, however, her footsteps slowed. She noticed greyish fur on the man's hands. His hair was slicked back, revealing pointed, wolfish ears, which twitched. She recognized the frame in that fancy green overcoat.

The man spun. His eyes widened.

"Zeke?" Perle's heart swelled as she scanned him from head to toe. She had never seen him dressed so regally before. *Is he really a prince in disguise?*

Zeke swallowed. "Perle..."

Perle rushed to him, wrapping her arms around him in a tight embrace. "Zeke, I am so glad to see you tonight!" She nestled her head against his chest, and heard the thrumming of his fast-beating heart.

Zeke's body stiffened. "I... I didn't think you'd come," his voice cracked.

She slowly pulled away, and looked up at him, beaming. "That makes two of us. Does this mean... you want to go to the ball with me?"

He chewed his bottom lip, and then nodded once. "Yeah... Hey. I... I want to tell you something, Perle. I hope you don't take offense to it..."

She cocked her head to the side, noting the distress in his voice. She took his hands and held them tight. "I promise, I won't take offense. What is it you want to tell me?"

He squeezed her hands. "I... I like you, Perle. A lot. Maybe too much." He paused and clenched his jaw. "I'm in love with you."

She started. Her hands slowly fell away from his and she looked at him with disbelief. "Love? That... That's crazy. I mean, we're friends, right?" His words continued echoing through her mind. *Love...* Her heart beat faster. This man loved her? Zeke Wolfson loved her? Her mind swirled with mixed emotions. She truly admired and cared for him. He had been running away for so long, and now he was finally opening up his heart. Perle could not begin to understand this phenomenon.

Zeke frowned. "Yeah, I know. It's crazy. I just needed to get it off my chest. Other than Ms. Fay and the Headmistress, you're the only one who's really cared, despite my... stubbornness.

You're still willing to talk to me, even when I try to push you away. And you saved my life all those months ago when we first encountered Tilda. There's so much about you that I'm grateful for. I love you, Perle Durand. I've never said those words before to anyone. I just wanted you to know how I felt."

Her eyes burned. "Zeke... I don't know what to say."

"You don't have to say anything. In fact, I'm not expecting you to. I understand you don't feel the same way. I wasn't exactly much of a good friend to you..."

She took his hands again. "What are you talking about? You've been a great friend. You've protected me, and you've helped others. You're a little rough around the edges, but that's okay. I like you the way you are. I was hoping you would ask me to the ball, because, well... I smile when I think about you. I find myself always worrying about you, and I don't know why... well, maybe I do now. Maybe it is love, Zeke."

His eyebrows rose slightly. "You would love me like this? A… cursed monster?"

Perle smiled. "Why not? My mother did, and I think she did pretty good taking that gamble."

He mirrored her smile. "Yeah, she did, and now she has the most beautiful daughter in the world."

"Thank you…" The tears welling in her eyes finally rolled down her burning cheeks. *Poetic, noble, honorable… He is no monster.* She rose on her tiptoes and planted a gentle kiss on his furry cheek. "I love you, too, Zeke Wolfson," she whispered, warmth and happiness spreading through her veins.

Zeke shuddered. A dim, purple glow emanated around him, then became brighter. Zeke groaned and sank to his knees. Soon, he was encompassed in a bright, white light.

Perle gasped and shielded her eyes with the back of her hand. *No! Zeke!* She reached out blindly toward him. Zeke growled and screamed, his voice a mix of human and wolf. Suddenly, the light disappeared. Perle slowly lowered her hand from her face. Zeke was curled in a fetal position on the ground, panting.

She gasped and rushed to his side. "Zeke! Are you okay?"

Zeke grunted, then sat up slowly. His face was human again, the fur on his body gone. The curse was lifted. And thankfully, the transformation hadn't destroyed his clothes this time. He felt his face and his eyes went wide. He scrambled over to the nearby fountain and peered at his reflection. He exhaled in surprise. "The curse. It's gone!" He beamed.

She mirrored his smile. *"Merveilleuse!* I'm so happy!" She hugged him again. This time, she didn't feel his body tense.

Zeke stared deep into her eyes. "You saved me, yet again..." He paused a beat, then slowly brought his face closer to hers.

Her heart pounded faster as his face inched closer. Her unconditional love for Zeke amplified. She met him halfway, and their lips crashed hard. The kiss was deep, passionate, and magical. *If this is a dream, I never want to awaken,* she thought, melting into his kiss, inhaling his scent.

Finally, Zeke pulled away, and he looked at her with hooded eyes. "Perle Durand, I want to take you to the ball tonight."

She gave his hand an eager squeeze. Her first ball would indeed be a memorable one. A magical night like no other with her one true love. "Lead the way."

ABOUT THE AUTHOR

MARIE LONG is an award-winning novelist who enjoys the snowy weather, the mountains, and a cup of hot white chocolate. She's an avid supporter of literacy movements. To learn more about her, visit her website: www.marielongauthor.com.

www.ingramcontent.com/pod-product-compliance
Lightning Source LLC
Chambersburg PA
CBHW030821210726
48290CB00002B/704